In the Wake of Night

Hollie Furniss

Published by Hollie Furniss, 2023.

IN THE WAKE OF NIGHT

First edition. April 6, 2023.

ISBN: 979-8215640548

Written by Hollie Furniss.

Prologue

1998

Such an angelic face. How I long to stroke your chalk-white skin with my fingertips. Feel the soft ridges of your perfect profile. Caress the gentle slope of your freckled nose and the plump of your cheek. To trace your protruding cupid's bow that shines irresistibly in the amber glow. If only I could part those supple, rosy lips with a kiss. Your brow is frowning. What is on your mind? I wish I could banish all your worries away. Just look at me. Open your chestnut-brown eyes and look at me. If only you could see how beautiful you are through my gaze. A murmur. A stir. You are so restless tonight aren't you? Do you want me to slide beneath your sheets? I could hold your precious body against mine. Hug the curves of your waist between my hands. Whisper your name in your ear. Sophia. Could you resist me? Don't turn away. I long to pull you back into view. Alas, I shall leave you to your dreams. Until tomorrow, my love.

Chapter One

1991

"I can't believe no one heard anything!" Francis explodes.

My parents are quieter, "Shhh. Lucas is still asleep. I don't want to scare him."

My ears prick up at the sound of my name. What's going on? I roll out of bed and rub my blinking eyes. One of my pyjama legs is uncomfortably rolled up higher than the other. I hate it when that happens. I head to the landing and lean quietly over the stairs to get a better listen.

Someone sobs, "We need to call the police. Francis, don't touch anything. You might damage evidence."

It sounds like my mum. Why do we need to call the police? I tip-toe down the stairs, careful not to make a sound. Peeking through the spindles on my descent, I notice that my mum, dad, and sister huddle together in the sitting room. Except, the room doesn't look like it normally does. Papers, drawers, and cushions litter the floor. My mum's bag sprawls open and empty on the varnished coffee table. Our TV no longer perches on the corner cabinet. To the side, I spot a discoloured, faded square where a radio once lived. None of mum's favourite figurines stand along the mantlepiece, as they had done the day before. As I scan the room, something catches my eye. In front of the window, the curtains billow. The window is wide open.

They don't hear my approach. "What's going on?" I ask.

Their eyes flash in my direction, "Oh Lucas! We've been burgled," my mum motions me to her, "don't touch anything."

I run into her arms. Someone was in our house. A thought worms its way into my subconscious. Did they come to my room?

My dad's hand strokes my matted hair, "Did you see or hear anything dear?"

I think back to the night. A dreamless sleep. Uninterrupted. I lift my head to look dad straight in the face. "No, I didn't." Would they come back?

After the police had been and taken statements from each of us, I go back to my room. My sanctuary. Opening the door, a flood of comforting aqua fills my vision. Light pours in through the window. The odd chugging of cars can be heard from the street outside. My matching blue single bed is pushed up against the wall, right under the opened window. I nestle in and peer out, trying to imagine how different the road would have looked last night. No one would know such a crime took place. People cycle aimlessly on their bikes up and down the slick pavement. Children laugh on the corner as they play games like hopscotch. Older kids likely remain indoors glued to their Sega. Typical, humdrum Roseville suburbia.

I know the stealing part is terrible. Now I am over the shock, I keep coming back to the idea of someone lurking inside unnoticed. Undeterred. They floated silently through my house like a ghost. Evading the capture of my mum, who catches me in a lie without even taking a second breath.

Eluding my dad, a man who knows someone's feelings with a single glance. Francis on the other hand sleepwalks through life. In the day, she doesn't care what people do, so it makes complete sense she didn't hear a damn thing. At sixteen, her interests consist of two things: which boys like her and how she can best maintain her appearance to keep it that way. I nearly forgot, make those three things. She also plays *I Like the Way* on repeat. Best put Hi-Five on the list too. If they robbed us, she would know.

I, on the other hand, have hardly any hobbies. Nothing that people my age can relate to anyway. As much as I tease my sister, at least she is a normal girl who does normal things; hang out with her friends at shopping malls, gets giddy over the lead guy in chick-flicks, or has a tantrum when she can't have the latest fashion craze.

I just don't fit in. I know at eight years old I have plenty of time to grow, but I just don't feel like the rest of the boys in my class. I find it hard to make friends, always have. There is so much pressure. Just thinking about it accelerates my heartbeat. Emotions aside, the chitchat doesn't even interest me either. All their concerns seem so mediocre, so boring. I don't like football – or any other sport. I don't do comic books or superheroes. Pop music is horrendous and don't get me started on the TV shows people my age enjoy. I'm like an adult in a child's body. Perhaps I was somebody else in another life? Maybe from the 1920s. Something I do enjoy is Ernest Hemingway and F.Scott Fitzgerald. My favourite book though has to be The Catcher in the Rye by Salinger. I identify so much with Holden. In fact, I think he's my hero. He's just so honest.

I fling my head against the softness of my pillow and continue to ruminate. Whoever did crawl through the downstairs window, was stealthy and brave – like Holden. They must have been seasoned burglars. How long would it take someone to learn a skill like that? I don't want to steal anything, no, but I can't escape the curiosity building inside me. What would it feel like to be able to invade someone's home without capture?

Chapter Two

1992

I start small. The lack of landing light signals everyone is residing to their beds, so I wait. How long will it take a household to fall into a deep sleep? I figure an hour will suffice, so I list my ploys. Just writing about the things I could do feels exciting. Although, to anyone on the outside they would sound pretty mundane. The difference here is they have no place during the night.

Knowing my house like the palm of my hand, I avoid the creaking floorboards. A flashlight illuminates my path down the staircase. I am careful to move slow and steady. It is only when I reach the living room that I notice I've been holding my breath. This is *my* house, I *live* here. If I get caught, I could just say I was sleepwalking. I notice my tense shoulders relax at my internal thoughts. No longer stiff, my legs loosen. I am ready for my mission.

The glaring white-light fans out across the kitchen floor, guiding me closer to my target. I place my hand on its shiny, smooth surface and pull. The fridge's seal breaks, letting out a soft ripping sound that I've never noticed before. Condiment jars rattle as I open it wider. Would that be loud enough to wake someone? I turn my flashlight off now that I bathe in the fluorescent glow of the fridge. It hums knowingly at me. A comforting sound. What did I fancy? If mum were around, she'd tell me off for letting all the cold air escape as I ponder. A peanut butter sandwich. That's what I'll make.

Taking out the peanut butter, I settle it gradually down on the countertop. The bread bin lid eases up in my hand, releasing an earthy, malty odour. I pull open the cutlery draw just wide enough to reach a knife. I can't reach the plates without climbing on the kitchen side, so instead, I just take one from the drying rack by the dripping sink. Now I have everything I need.

I unscrew the peanut butter lid and scoop out some of the sticky goodness with my knife. After spreading it finely across both slices of bread, I cut the sandwich into triangles. Staring back at my masterpiece, I reflect, if there was a contest for the longest sandwich-making process, I would win.

I potter over to a dining chair, cautious not to scratch the legs along the vinyl and take a bite. This is the best sandwich I've ever made.

Once I tidy up the evidence of my midnight snack, I make it back to the top of the stairs. I pause and listen. All I can hear are my dad's snores. Nothing else. I've done it. Triumphantly, I re-enter my bedroom and consider what sandwich I will make tomorrow.

There are only so many sandwiches a boy can make. Each night I've been pushing myself further, seeing how much I can do. In the first week of leading this double life, the only indication that something was amiss was my tiredness during the day. I began napping after dinner, claiming to be doing homework instead. This has really improved my stamina and alertness. Now, when the sun sets, I'm ready to claim the night.

I can't explain how peaceful it is. Knowing you are truly alone with your thoughts. I know people are still around me but consciously they are in another world. I've learnt so much about my family too.

Watching my parents sleep, I've noticed how my mother embraces my father. She snuggles down behind him, practically a heap under the duvet. All I see is the tip of her wiry hair. It is strange to see them so close considering that I've never seen them kiss or hug before. My father mumbles profanity he'd never allow me to hear normally. I haven't heard or seen him show any sign of a temper. It's like he bottles it all up and the bad words slip out involuntarily as he drifts. I get to see my sister without makeup! When she's resting, I actually like her. She looks like she did when she was just a kid. Innocent. Sweet. I find myself remembering memories I thought I'd forgotten as I stare into her expressionless face. Times when we were happy enough to play with one another. Young enough to know no different. I look around her room and her wallpaper of magazine cut-outs and polaroid pictures with melancholy. When did we become so distant?

Tonight, I need more. My night unfolds like usual. The clock strikes twelve and I creep out of bed (already dressed in daywear). I take my navy backpack from under my bed and check that I have everything I will need. Flashlight, check. Binoculars, check. Chocolate bar, check. Note pad, check. Pen, check.

You see, in the hours leading up to my family's slumber, I have begun spying on my neighbours. I kneel on my bed and adjust my blinds just enough for my binoculars to poke through. By twelve, most of the houses on my street are blacked out. Curtains drawn. Lights off. As good as my binoculars are, I urge to get nearer.

My feet dance down the stairs, dodging any loose floorboards that would groan under my weight. Butterflies flutter in my stomach as I softly unlock the front door. Before going any further, I listen. This game is mostly about waiting. Nothing stirs, so I take the door handle between my fingers and turn. The door releases with a subtle squeak. Again I pause like a frozen statue. Content nobody heard a thing, I close the door behind me and exhale. My breath smokes in the night air, and my senses heighten. I search left to right for any signs of life. The street is heavy with quietness. The only distant sound is the croak of a bird, calling to the moon.

I stick to the pavements, glancing around as I strut. At the end of the street, I spot a silhouette behind an illuminated curtain. Just like in movies, the figure appears to be undressing. Black arms criss-cross up and over their head and discard a top somewhere out of view. They are slender and tall like a model. With swishes of shoulder-length hair, I imagine she's female. Her age baffles me. Unlike my mother, she has no lumps or bumps. Perhaps she is examining her body in front of a mirror. Suddenly, she turns on her heel and retreats away from my vantage point.

Seeking stimulation, I prowl across the road. As I approach the house opposite mine, I hear a clanking of metal. My legs stop dead on the spot and my heart drops. I've been caught.

The rustling commences once again but this time even louder. My hands clutch the straps of my backpack tight as I turn round. A fox glares back at me with iridescent eyes, as he stands still amid a toppled bin. My breathing steadies just as it darts off in a blur of orange fur. Above me, curtains begin to twitch. Lights flicker. I press my body up against the nearest house and hide behind a hedge. My mind races with questions. What's the penalty for snooping? How angry would someone be if they found me lurking in their garden? Could I claim to be running away from home?

While my knees ache from crouching, people begin to settle back into bed. The street reclaims its silence. I remain uncaught. The thrill of such a notion is euphoric. Goosebumps prickle across my skin. I know that I've found my new hunting ground. The confinement of my own home is no longer enough.

Chapter Three

1998

The smell of toast and freshly brewed coffee fills the kitchen. My mum flurries around the dining table, setting out breakfast plates. I'm dreading heading back to school after the Holidays. All the festivities are over, decorations packed away. January is such a bleak month.

"Hurry up Lucas, you don't want to be late and neither do I!"

Mum works as an English Teacher at Sacramento Charter High School, where I attend as a sophomore. Although, nobody realises. My mother has never taken my father's last name. Mrs Walker is her title. Thankfully, she doesn't teach the 10th Grade. I insist on her dropping me off around the corner from school so that I don't have the embarrassment of being seen together. I've worked extremely hard on drawing as little attention as possible, and I don't intend for that to end anytime soon.

"Hello? Earth to Lucas? Can you hear me? Get some breakfast down you, pronto. We leave in ten."

The buttered toast crunches between my fingers as I chew. Donned in a pale suit, my father wanders through the doorway.

"Morning, kiddo. Ready for your first day back?" he asks in his chirpy, morning voice.

"Ready as I'll ever be," I mumble, my mouth filled with bread.

"That's my boy, fake it 'till you make it!"

I start loading my bag with schoolbooks and stationery by the front door, still in earshot of the kitchen. I overhear my mum informing my dad about the recently purchased house across the road.

"Have you heard Jim, the new neighbours will be moving in later today. I wonder what they'll be like?"

"Oh that's great, I'm sick of seeing that garden overgrown. We should invite them round for dinner, introduce them to the street."

"That's a great idea. They might even have children Lucas's age. I'll keep an eye out for new pupils today."

The thought of strangers coming over for dinner fills me with fear. I cough loudly, indicating my readiness (and desire to stop discussing such matters). Mum takes the hint and begins putting on her forest-green parka. We venture out in the brisk morning air. Cold bites at my fingertips as we make our way to the silver Ford. Settling in, I turn my attention to the scenery out of the window. The radio crackles with country music, my mum's favourite. Outside, people of all shapes and sizes go about their daily commutes. Unaware of my glare through the transparent glass. The trees are still bare and naked, in the midst of winter. Everyone wraps up warm against the bitter chill. By midday, we will all be shedding our coats. The weather here warms up quickly. Before I know it, we reach my pitstop.

"See you later darling, have a lovely day."

"You too mum," I call back, over the creak of the car door.

I blend into the flock of people making their way to school. With my head down, my overgrown hair dangles in my eyes. I despise the hairdressers so suffer through it. Inside the school halls, I make my way to my locker. Nearby, a group of friends screech as they reunite. I've never understood such banal behaviour. Pulling out my timetable, I see my first class is Chemistry. The bell rings and homeroom beckons.

Inside the rectangular classroom, I look at my classmates' faces. Girls caked in cosmetics, guys beginning to grow stubble, and then I notice a new face. A face unlike anyone else in the room. She sits fidgeting in her seat, pulling at her skirt and blouse. Her skin void of foundation is milky white. Bold, brown eyes dart around the place, taking everything in. She bites briefly against her bottom lip and tucks her long hair behind her ears, yet to notice me.

"Good morning all, and welcome back. I hope you all enjoyed your Holiday break and are looking forward to getting back into your studies," Mr Morris says with hands thrust into his brown, corduroy trouser pockets.

A grumble erupts across the room.

"Before we take the register, I wanted to start by introducing a new member of Sacramento Charter High School. Let's all give a warm welcome to, Sophia Andrews."

Mr Morris indicates towards the new girl in question as the class clap at her arrival. She smiles nervously and gives the class a subtle wave, practically under her desk. I wonder what her interests are and where she's come from. As if reading my mind, Mr Morris continues.

"Sophia joins us all the way from Richmond. To help Miss Andrews familiarise herself with the school I need a volunteer. Someone who wouldn't mind giving her a tour of the school premises and taking her to each of her classes this week." Mr Morris scans the room. Nobody moves an inch. "Anyone?"

I raise my hand. Sophia's gaze finally rests on mine.

"Oh...Lucas. Excellent! The job is yours."

After registration, Sophia makes her way towards me. My heart thumps hard in my chest.

"Thanks for offering to help me this week. For a moment there, I thought nobody would," she laughs self-consciously as she squeezes her hands.

Up close, she looks even more pretty. I turn to the floor, not wanting to stare. As I inhale, I take her in. Sophia has a flowery, tropical scent. I lick my lips instinctively.

"Sure. It's no bother. What is your first class?"

"Math. You?"

"Chemistry. Math is on route though, I can walk you."

I lead Sophia down the maze of corridors and call out key landmarks to help her find her way. The cotton of her blouse brushes against my arm as we snake around the corner. I close my eyes for a second, surprised by the sensation.

"Here we are. I'll come and meet you here afterwards to take you to your next lesson. I'm just down the hall."

"Great. I'll wait for you."

Our faces are inches away from one another. Still, I avoid direct eye contact and fixate on her sneakers.

"Perfect. See you then."

As I march towards Chemistry, I hear her thank me and wonder if she can hear my sigh of relief.

Luckily for me, I am years ahead of the curriculum and already know all I need to know on the subject of Stoichiometry. This allows me to daydream during class. You don't need to be Albert Einstein to know the focus of my attention. Sophia fascinates me. I replay the events that had just unfolded and worry about how I may have come across. I've never really interacted with anyone, let alone a girl. Sophia is different though. She is a little strange like me. Uncharacteristically lowkey and timid. I just hope that she doesn't get caught up in one of Sacramento's social cliques.

When Chemistry finally ends, I shuffle alongside the outpouring of pupils. The feeling radiating through my veins feels familiar. Excitement embroiled with nerves. I head straight to Sophia's Math class, mentally preparing myself for the social pressures that await. Through the sea of floating heads, I spot her. Leaning against the magnolia wall, nibbling at her cuticles, waiting for me.

"Good lesson?" I enquire.

"So, so. Math really isn't my strong suit."

"Where next?"

"Art, something I actually like."

So she's the creative type. The yin to my yang.

"That's cool. I like art, I'm just no good at it myself."

We set off, strolling side-by-side. Her fine hair swishes behind her. My nostrils fill once again with her sweet, delectable scent.

"What are you good at?" she asks.

Do I respond honestly and risk coming off as arrogant? The truth is I'm good at most things academic. The truth is I'm good at spying on people.

"I like writing best. It is just a shame the types of books we cover are tripe."

"I wish I could write. I think I have dyslexia or something. None of it comes naturally to me. With Art, I don't need to think. It is just effortless. That's why I love it."

She grins as she talks and her nose wrinkles when she gets passionate. It's adorable. I'd give anything to see her artwork. We halt outside of the studio, and I stall, not wanting to leave her just yet.

"Maybe you can show me your work some time, if you want?"

"I didn't say I was any good. I just enjoy it. Is this my stop?"

"Yes, I'll meet you next for lunch. I'll take you to the cafeteria."

"Will you sit with me? I'd hate to be alone on my first day."

Would she want to eat with me if she knew how I dine solo, day after day?

"Of course."

When we do unite for lunch, I learn Sophia is quite a private person. I ask her about life back in Richmond, but she seems reluctant to expand. This only peaks my interest even more. The bombshell I do learn is that she has in fact moved into the house across from me in Roseville. The idea comes to me instantaneously when the opportunity arises.

"Shoot, I forgot my water. I'll just be a sec," she says in the middle of lunch.

"No problem, I'll keep your seat."

As she runs over to the counter, I see she's left her bag behind. The temptation is too strong to ignore. I reach over and rummage around, feeling for the hard metal. Sensing the rough edges of her keys, I take them in one swoop and pocket them in my jeans. Sophia jogs back to our table, water in hand.

"So, you were telling me about Roseville. What's there to do for fun?"

Unbeknownst to her, the type of fun I like is illicit. We continue like this sharing small talk and I feel that I've made a friend. My first and only friend. Even though she sits living and breathing in front of me now, I can't help but visualise her lying in bed. Asleep.

Chapter Four

I skip physical education and head to the local locksmiths, which is around a 20-minute stroll. As predicted, the weather has warmed, so I tie my coat around my waist. The grey streets are practically empty as I pound the pavement. I like the peace and quiet at this hour. Most people are busy at school or at work.

Soon enough, the land begins to incline and I'm huffing up a hill, with sweat building at my brow. I catch myself giggling aloud at the notion of my struggle, considering that I'm bunking gym.

The shop front shines against the winter sun, enticing me in. A jangling of bells ring upon my entry. The shop looks dim compared to the whiteness of the outside. I scan around the cluttered space. An oversize, bald man with sprouting nose hair greets me.

"Good afternoon, what can I do you for?"

I pull the keys from my pocket. They take a bit of wiggling before finally succumbing to my grasp.

"I need a key cut, please."

"Just the one? We have an offer of three keys for the price of two."

"Just the one is fine, thanks."

The man behind the counter sniffles and rubs his hairy nose, before taking the key from me. I'll have to disinfect them before I return them to Sophia.

"It won't take very long. Take a seat."

The waiting area consists of two worn, distressed faux leather seats. Old magazines sandwich between them, so I take a gander. In a matter of minutes, the key is cut, and I pay him using the loose change in my coat. As easy as that, I reflect, on my way back into the daylight. A smirk plastering my face.

When I make it back to school, Sophia loiters in the mahogany hallway.

"Good day?" I call from afar, closing the gap with each stride.

"Yes, thank you," she says unconvincingly while scratching her head, "What's next for you?"

"I help with the Student Newspaper but not today."

"Well then, it seems pointless walking back home separately. Seems as we live so close to one another."

"Right. Just give me one minute. I'll be right back."

Not wanting to pass up an opportunity to spend more time with Sophia, I run to my mum's classroom, and let her know I won't be needing a lift.

"Who are you walking home with?" she questions.

"Sophia, she is our new neighbour. I'm her assigned buddy for the week."

My mum's face beams. This is the first time I've ever mentioned a girl.

"That's wonderful, Lucas. Invite her and her family over for dinner, tonight. I'd love to get to know her too."

I finally manage to escape my mum and catch up with Sophia. We set off on our long walk home. She is the first to break the silence.

"What do you write about?"

"Pardon?"

"For the Student Newspaper?"

"Oh, I don't. I actually help with the photography."

I spend most of our journey discussing my work and favourite photographers: Man Ray and André Kertész for reference. I adore the nuances of Noire et Blanche and the aerial composition of Window Views. Sophia admits she doesn't know all that much about the subject but finds it interesting. Although, she could just be saying that to humour me.

At the foot of her front garden, I pluck up the courage to invite her to dinner.

"I'll have to check with my parents first. They'll let you know."

Just as she turns to walk down her path, I kneel on the floor with her keys in my hand.

"Did you drop these?"

"I didn't even hear them fall. Strange."

I pass them to her as she thanks me.

"Or if your parents prefer, we could come round to yours and help you unpack?"

Sophia's eyes widen. Her hand rests against the brass handle, making her bag slump down her arm, towards the patio.

"Great idea. I'll be sure to put that to them. Thanks again for today," she replies, as she retreats inside and closes the door.

Getting a feel for the layout of the house will be advantageous. That way, I can better prepare.

Chapter Five

Without a doubt, I am surprised to hear the Andrews have invited my parents and me for drinks however the overarching emotion is undeniably, anticipation. Wanting to make a good impression, I put on a fresh sweater and attempt to flatten and mould my wavy mane. I stare back at my appearance in the smeared mirror behind my door. Was I attractive? I focus on the prominence of my nose, dominating my face. Dark irises almost merge with the blackness of my pupils. Dry skin has built up on my lips and I begin to pick at their edges, causing them to bleed. At fifteen years of age, I've never been kissed. This is down to two reasons. First, I've never been in a situation where kissing would even come into the equation. No dates, no sleepovers, no parties. None of that has ever entered my orbit. Second, I've never met someone that has made me think about kissing. Sure, I've felt drawn to women, their aura. It is like appreciating art. I would look, but I would not touch.

My mum calls from downstairs, freeing me from the depths of my mind. It is time. To make this moment count, I need to ensure I take some essentials. A slight notebook, smaller than A5 just fits into my back pocket. As does my stunted pencil.

"Hurry up, Lucas. We don't want to be late," my dad echoes.

We make our way across the road, with the smell of perfume trailing our path. An older woman opens the door to welcome us before we make it off the pavement. She introduces herself as Janice, Sophia's mum, and tells us to mind the mess. She has a look of Sophia with limp hair and brown eyes, but her features are sunken and creased. Sophia's dad towers next to her. He shakes our hands with a firm grip before escorting us to their living room. I spy the rim of Sophia's spindly legs as we enter. She sits, rather proper, with her legs together and crossed hands resting neatly on her thighs.

After introducing ourselves and greeting one another, we all sit together on their cream sofas. The house looks pretty well organised, considering they'd just moved it.

"You've made such a great start on the house, Janice," my mum gushes.

"You think? Fred and I took the whole day off to unpack. We just love it here already."

As Janice and my mum gossip over interior design, Fred instructs Sophie.

"Make our guests some drinks, love."

Following his direction, she takes our orders and swiftly returns with a tray of beverages. Mine being the cola. When my dad strikes up a conversation with Fred, I turn to Sophia and smile. I notice, she has changed her attire from earlier to a turquoise green jumper and denim jeans. Her hair looks freshly brushed too. Is that for me?

"So you like it here then?"

"Yeah, it's great. Better than Richmond anyway. This move is meant to be a fresh start. A clean slate."

"A fresh start from what?"

My mother suddenly interrupts our discussion, "Sophia, how was your first day at school? I hear Lucas has been assigned as your buddy. I hope he's been helpful."

I scan the room as she replies, talking about her various lessons and teachers. It dawns on me; the layout of the house is almost identical to my house. Jackpot. How about the upstairs though?

"Where's the bathroom?" I ask.

Sophia leads me upstairs and I am careful to feel for any creaks. 1,2,3... creak,4,5,6,7,8... creak,9,10,11,12... creak. The steps are imprinted in my frontal lobe.

"What?" Sophia says.

I must have been mumbling aloud. I think on my feet.

"Erm, no siblings then?"

"Sadly not. You?"

"A sister but she's shacked up with her fiancé."

"Lucky her."

She motions towards the toilet door at the top of the stairs.

"Here we are. I'll meet you back downstairs."

Inside the lavatory, I pull out my pad and pencil and make a note of my observations so far. Flushing the toilet and leaving the tap to run, I venture out onto the landing. Footprint wise, Sophia's room is the same as the one my sister had. Makes sense, considering it is a larger bedroom. The equivalent of my room is currently being used as a dumping ground for boxes and bags. I long to explore further but restrain myself. Tonight, I muse.

Back in the living room, the conversation is still fractured. People are broken up in separate chats. I join the one with Fred, my father and Sophia.

"So, what are your interests, Lucas?" Fred questions as I approach.

I inform him about my photography and love of literature, much to his dismay. He tells me straight off the bat, it is odd for a young boy my age to not being interested in sport.

"I was on the soccer squad back in my day, midfielder – could have gone professional too, if it weren't for Sophia coming along. Blessing in disguise really."

An uncomfortable grin forms on Sophia's face. She doesn't like the spotlight either. We continue like this for another hour or so, then call it a night. I take one last glance around on our way to the front door. The cabinets are already dressed in photographs of the family. I make a mental note to take a closer look later. My watch ticks past eight o'clock. Four hours and counting.

Chapter Six

Stars beam bright against the ink-blue sky. A soft hush breathes through the houses as the wind blows. Streetlamps glare over parked cars, casting their silhouettes along the concrete. Her house stands in the shadows. My hands twitch with wonder. What does Sophia look like at this moment? What is she thinking, feeling? I flip the key over in my hand, pressing the sharp edge into my palm before turning it over onto its flat surface. Over and over. I think back to the break-in at my home all those years ago. The same adrenaline that they must have felt, pumps through my blood now. I can't help but feel a sense of bonding. We are somehow intertwined and bound together by this obscure common interest. Is it power or desperation that drives us?

Since being a little boy, I have been consumed by a need to see the unseen. Know the unknown. Like an addict, over time, my impulses have grown more dangerous. I've become tolerant, desensitised and in need of a bigger hit. Tonight, I knowingly graduate from cocaine to heroin. I stare at the impending threshold. The desire takes over and I succumb. Not taking any chances, I remove my shoes and put them in my backpack. Socks will be far quieter. As the key twists in the lock, I pause to catch my breath. My heart throbs in my throat as I close my eyes and open the door.

IN THE WAKE OF NIGHT

The scene is a routine I have practised many times, back at my own house, but the sensation of unlocking someone else's door is so very different. The air is thick with trepidation. I practically wade through it to transition fully inside. There to greet me, are the framed photographs I spotted this evening. I pick one up and focus my flashlight on the image. A young Sophia stares back at me in a gingham dress and open-toe sandals. I settle the photograph back on the cabinet and illuminate the rest. All of them include Sophia, at varying stages of her life. In those with her parents, she affectionately leans against her father's chest or holds his hand. Daddy's little girl. In my favourite, Sophia and her mum are laid in a field with their hair splayed out, caught in a fit of laughter. What a warm, happy family unit they are. Could my life have been so effortless if I had been more accepting? There is no question, I see the glass half-empty. Could Sophia be my glass half-full?

Sophia. So close, yet so far.

I glide up the stairs, forgoing the creaks that I'd located earlier. At the top, I listen to the house and wait for my eyes to adjust. Someone snores softly. As I pass beyond Janice and Fred's bedroom, the snores fade, indicating that Sophia is not the perpetrator. I reach Sophia's door and bask in her electrifying presence. An undeniable force, willing me to enter. My hand bends the handle and I venture in. My eyes take a second to see the room through the blackness. I begin to make out the shape of her desk and bed, in the far corner. A wardrobe leans against the righthand wall, and I can just make out where the window is. Eager for more, I tug on the blind's cord, parting it just enough to allow some streetlight to filter in. The room transforms with a blue, yellow tinge.

Sophia is laid facing the wall, undisturbed. Her hair spreads across the pillow and I watch her back subtly rise and fall, like a melodic wave. Without her face visible, I turn my attention to her desk. Laid atop are several books and a large sketchpad. Her artwork perhaps? Upon opening the book, my predictions are verified but not in the way that I thought. Her work is dramatic, abstract, and visceral. Bold, angry, black lines strike the page. Squiggles build to create the form of a woman, cowering on the floor. The visual repeats itself in various positions. Each time, the piece evokes a sense of despair and anguish. What inspired such harrowing drawings? What happened in Richmond? I wish I could reach out to Sophia and soothe her, but I know that is impossible. Doing so would sever any trust I have briefly established.

Tomorrow, I must conjure a way of getting Sophia to talk about her past, without letting on that I've seen her artwork. Of all the quandaries' I am in right now, this poses the largest threat.

Chapter Seven

"**I** dreamt of you last night," Sophia announces, and my heart practically skips a beat.

"Oh really?"

"Yeah, I was waving to you from my window, and you were looking right at me, but you wouldn't wave back. Strange huh?"

"That's odd," I laugh, "just for the record, I'd never ignore you."

We sit together on the school grounds, grass imprinting against our palms. The weather is milder today, so I figure we would take our lunch outdoors. Frothy clouds sail across the baby blue sky, creating pictures of animals.

"Have you ever played that game, where you try to see pictures in the clouds? Take that one there," I point straight above us, "doesn't it remind you of a rabbit? With the long ears."

Sophia squints and agrees with my observation. She spots a lion, just as I make out a monkey or cat. Something with a swooping tail anyway. In unison, we raise our hands to the sky in recognition of a heart. It causes our fingers to collide, just for a moment. Shock waves ripple through my core, and I retract my arm. Did she feel that too? She simply giggles and leans her head back against the wild lawn that's been left unkept due to the cooler season. I think back to her body lying under the covers last night, and the mysterious sketches on her dresser.

"We got cut short yesterday at your house when we were talking."

"Did we?"

"You mentioned something about a fresh start? What was so bad about Richmond?"

The atmosphere changes instantly. Sophia's arm tenses against mine as she takes a deep inhale. I stare up at the pale sky, waiting for her reply.

"Life was chaotic there, that's all. My parents were arguing a lot about work and money. My dad... erm... he doesn't cope well under pressure or stress. Hopefully, his new job will change all that."

I try to read between the lines but the picture she paints is fuzzy and grey. It's clear she won't elaborate further, so I close the door on the topic. For now. Sophia rolls onto her front and grabs a sherbet dip from her plastic tray. As she sucks on the fizzing candy, I attempt to continue to the conversation, testing the boundaries.

"What is Fred's new job?"

Sophia tells me that her dad works as a salesman for a shoe brand I'd never heard of and that he is setting up the brand here in Sacramento. Her mum, Janice, is a nurse and sometimes works nights. That might be a problem, for me.

"Jeez, that must be tough. What are her hours out of interest?"

"She'll work three days from 8 pm-8 am and sleep most of the day. Then she gets two days off in-between."

False alarm. That works just fine. One less soul to worry about.

"Are you close with your family?" Sophie asks after several minutes of calm. I'm taken aback by the directness, then reflect back on my own probing queries.

I clear my throat before speaking, "Honestly, I feel like the black sheep of my family. I've never really fit in."

In the distance, bells ring indicating the end of recess. We gather our belongings for class.

"I get that. I often feel that there's something wrong with me."

People flow around us, making their way back into school and yet as our eyes lock, it is as if time stands still. This girl is getting under my skin. We share so much in common. God, I wish I were normal. I wish this would be enough for me. In reality, I am nothing like Sophia. She is pure and white, and I am rotten and dark. She is a million times better than I will ever be. I should stop. But you and I both know, that isn't going to happen.

That night, I watch as Sophia writhes in bed, caught in a nightmare she cannot awake. It takes all my strength not to shake her from her demons. Who is she afraid of?

Chapter Eight

Night after night, I venture into Sophia's room and observe her in her most magnificent and vulnerable state. How I wish to photograph the moment but unfortunately the risk of her hearing the snap of my camera is too likely. Instead, I try to mentally preserve even the simplest of movements. The flicker of her eyelids during the deepest of dreams, how she tosses and turns creating odd shapes that should feel incredibly uncomfortable, and the murmurs and groans I can't quite decipher. All of it is magical. All of it is important. To me.

Why am I so obsessed? It is a question that plagues my thoughts. All I know is that it gives me a purpose, a reason to wake each day and continue living. If I had met someone like me along the way, if I had met someone period, then I might be different by now. I may have outgrown these inclinations, these curiosities. But no one has. Sure, people have tried, but that's the thing – they came to me and they always turned out to be a disappointment. Don't be mistaken, I am lonely, but it is a loneliness of my own making. However, I'd rather be lonely than fake. I've rather live my life alone than appease someone else's ideals.

This way, I get to spend time with Sophia without the burden of judgement. Between these four walls, we can simply enjoy one another's company, without the bullshit. Something that has surprised me though, is how keen I am to not only spend my night savouring her slumber but also to see her at school. The night has become a time of reflection for me, a place I can mull over our conversations and consider my future encounters. Her room is filled with talking points, things to help me get closer to Sophia – the version of her when she is awake and aware. For instance, her stuffed teddies indicate her fondness for animals, in particular pandas. When the topic of reincarnation came up, I informed her how I'd love to come back as a panda. She proceeded to explain all the wonderful characteristics of such creatures. I was impressed by her knowledge of the animal and pleasantly surprised that her admiration for them went past their apparent cuteness.

On another occasion, I discovered that she has a thing for Titanic, I presume Leonardo DiCaprio specifically, as a film poster of him is stuck up against her lavender walls. I have no interest in the movie myself, but when I saw the poster in her room, I went to see it at the cinema on my own. It stuns me how many people were crying as the rolling credits aired. Nether-the-less, it gave me tons of conversation starters. I still worry though that Jack is the epitome of her desire and how I look nothing like him.

Like my parents, I have learnt so much about Sophia. This evening, her hair ribbons across her forward, thick with sweat. If I didn't know her, I'd say she was sick with fever. Except, I do know her. I know that she's obsessed with sherbet dips and how they fizz on her tongue. I know that she always wears a tank top under her t-shirt just in case she ever spills anything down herself. I know that she blinks a lot when she is feeling uncomfortable. I know that she secretly checks her teeth in a handheld mirror after she eats. I know her favourite pyjamas are lilac with a deep purple trim, and that most nights she fights against the scenes that flicker behind her eyes.

Sophia gargles nonsense and yearns for her dream to stop. Without thinking, I find myself shushing her, ever so quietly.

"It's okay," I murmur under my breath.

Slowly, her body relaxes and settles. I ache to stroke her hair but resist. Watching her peaceful face return, I take pleasure in knowing my presence brings her some comfort. Janice, Sophia's mum, is on nights and I have recognised that it is on these occasions that Sophia's nightmares are at their worst. As I sit, cross-legged on the wooden floor contemplating the enigma that is Sophia, I hear the scrape of a door. Suddenly, the gap under Sophia's bedroom door illuminates. Fred is awake.

The groan of the landing quakes gently as he proceeds towards Sophia's room, his footsteps blocking portions of the slivering light as he moves. Panic rises in my chest, and I frantically scan the room for an escape. With barely any time to think, I simply shuffle myself under Sophia's bed and blend into the shadows. With my head tilted to the side, I see the bedroom door swing open and Fred's bare feet stood still between the doorframe. Although I can't see his face, I imagine him searching the room, looking for the intruder. For me. I had lulled Sophia so softly even she didn't wake, but somehow Fred was aware. Visions of him clawing at me and dragging me from under the bed raced through my head. What would Sophia think of me?

Lost in my thoughts, I almost miss Fred walking forwards, towards me. Instinctively, I hold my breath tight and squeeze my eyes shut, waiting for Fred's hand to descend on my arm. It does not come. My eyes open wide to the sound of the mattress squeaking and the bed pressing further onto my body. Fred is in Sophia's bed. After a few seconds, Sophia's lilac pyjamas land on the floor next to me. The realisation of what is happening dawns with rising dread. My limbs begin to shake uncontrollably as I squirm under the pressure and sounds of the creaking mattress. I cover my mouth with my hand to muffle the scream building in my throat. It feels like being trapped inside a coffin filled with all your worst fears. There is nothing I can do but yearn and will it to stop, without speaking, out of the stupendous fear of getting caught and what that might mean.

I don't know how much time has passed, but the bed finally stops moving. Fred's naked feet hit the floor with a thump. He walks back to the door he had previously stood at, prowling, and closes it behind him. My head turns and stares at the back of the mattress, knowing Sophia lays only inches away. Her cries sound like she's holding back. Long pauses of silence break-up her gasping sobs, as she recoils from the pain. A single tear glides down my cheek. As much as I want to cry out and tell Sophia all I have witnessed, I know that I cannot. She would never forgive me. All I can do is press my hand against the base of her bed and weep alongside her, knowing that she is not alone. I am with her and somehow, I will protect her.

Chapter Nine

At school the next day, Sophia barely speaks. Dark, purple circles cup her eyes, and she seems vacant like she's sleepwalking through the day. Her fragile state makes her feel younger and even more petite. I know that tonight her mum will work another nightshift. Flashes of the likely event that will follow flicker behind my lids. I cannot let it happen again. As we sit facing one another at lunch, I strike up a conversation, attempting to pull her from the depths of her memories.

"So, I was thinking, we could start a study club."

Sophia frowns but for the first time all day, she is present.

"A study club?"

"Yeah, we could hang out after school and do our homework together. I can help you with Math and you can help me with…"

My brain searches for a subject Sophia has more expertise with. As I languish in the struggle, she chirps up, "Art?"

"Yes, Art!" I say, practically shouting, "And perhaps other things too, like helping me… socially."

"If you haven't noticed Lucas, I'm not that great at making friends either, you're all I have."

I let the sentence linger in the air. I'm all she has.

"Trust me, you are." I eventually respond.

Sophia leans her head to one side and lifts her eyebrows.

"Study club?"

"Study club." I parrot back, firmly.

She finally accepts the idea, and we plan to meet at her house tonight after dinner. We return to picking at our lunches before the bell rings out. I notice that Sophia has left almost all of her lunch. I make a mental note to bring snacks to our first study club meeting later.

"What shall we call it? Our study club," I ask as we march down the halls to class.

Sophia clutches her books against her chest as if they are sacred. I can tell she is thinking hard as she bites her lip, the way she did the first time I ever laid eyes on her.

"Is The Misfits too on the nose?"

We both burst out laughing. People stare at us contemplating what we think is so funny. My chuckle ends before Sophia's, and I rejoice at the sound of her giggle. She has a robust, energetic laugh like a full and heady red wine. It is truly dazzling. I wish I could make her happy like this every day.

We part our ways outside of Home Economics and the sadness returns to Sophia's face. For the first time, I stop imagining her asleep in bed and fantasize about her lying next to me, smiling and free. Before I can hesitate, I reach out and hug her. Her books press against me, digging into my ribs, but I don't care. I hold her and drink in every second. At first, she feels rigid between my arms. Stiff. It doesn't take her long to soften and sink into my embrace. When I let her go, I simply smile and walk away, knowing how much that hug would mean to her at that moment. Even though I don't look back, I can feel Sophia stood behind me, starring.

After school, I continuously watch the clock as I funnel food into my mouth.

"Lucas, you are eating like you're feral. Did you not have much at lunch?" my mum asks.

I wipe the spaghetti juices from my mouth and reply, cheeks still full of pasta, "It is just so delicious."

My mum smiles at this and stops badgering me about my haste. I swallow the lump of food and announce my evening plans, "Sophia and I are going to start doing our homework together. I'm heading to hers tonight to help her with her Maths."

My parents share glances with each other. I wonder what they are more surprised at. The fact that I am hanging out with someone outside of school or that I am meeting up with a girl. Alone.

"That's great boyo. You'll make a fantastic tutor," my dad says with a smirk.

I practically lick my plate clean and excuse myself from the table. Upstairs, I grab my backpack containing all my stationery and the addition of sweets, including Sophia's favourite. Dashing out of the house, my parents wish me good luck. It feels strange heading to Sophia's house in the light of day after so long of sneaking about under the guise of nightfall. I knock on the door, excited. Then I see him and abruptly remember.

"Afternoon Lucas. Study club aye? Sophia's told me all about it. Sounds like a great idea. She certainly needs the help," Fred declares upon opening the front door.

The hatred that pulsates through my body is venomous. I thought I knew hate, but the feelings I had about things before last night pales in comparison to how I feel now. This hate is pure and intense. Focused. I attempt to shimmer its heat as I reply, "Is Sophia ready?"

Fred tells me to head on up. Janice hasn't departed yet so greets me by the stairs. I wonder if she really is clueless about what goes on between her husband and daughter. Then I think about how easily I have deceived people over the years. You don't expect the unexpected.

I stop at the top of the stairs at the sight of Sophia's bedroom door, knowing the steps I was about the take mirrored that of Fred last night. It made me almost sick. I shake off the nerves and think of Sophia. She needs me right now, and the less time she is alone in this house, the better. I approach her door and gently push it open. Perched on the end of her bed, Sophia beams back at me.

"Lucas! Welcome to my room. Mind the mess."

I find it amusing that she thinks this is my first encounter. I play along and pretend everything is new to me. She gives me the grand tour as she calls it and we finish sitting on her wooden floor, by her bed. The same spot I spend each night watching over her.

"So, where should we start?" she asks, tucking a strand of loose hair behind her ear.

I pull out the bag of sweets and chuck her the sherbet one. She tucks in impatiently. Distracted by the sugar, I use the moment to bring up something I've wanted her to discuss for some time.

"I was wondering, are you finally ready to show me your artwork yet?"

Sophia looks stunned, hurt. I worry I've ruined the mood. Everything was going so well. She takes a deep breath and heads to her desk to retrieve her sketchpad. She passes it to me but continues to hold one of its edges.

"I've never shown this to anyone, so this is a pretty big deal, okay?"

The sentiment is touching. I already know what illustrations lay etched onto the page, but the fact she is willingly entrusting me to look is huge.

"Okay," I simply reply, and feel her let go, allowing me to take it.

When I open the book, I scowl with confusion. This is not the same sketchpad that I perused weeks ago. There, glaring back at me is myself. I flick through the book and see page after page of my face drawn in incredible detail. On some, Sophia has replicated moments we've shared. My favourite is a drawing of us laid on the grass, side by side, pointing to the sky.

"They are amazing," I mutter quietly, almost lost for words.

"Before I came here, my drawings were... pretty morbid. Then I met you. You're my muse," she nudges me playfully as she speaks. I can't believe all this time I thought I was the one with the secrets. I never once stopped to consider Sophia as the dark horse.

"I don't know what to say, nobody has ever done anything like this for me. I didn't think I was interesting enough."

"I find you extremely interesting."

As I bring my gaze from the book to Sophia's eyes, I see them shine. How beautiful she is.

"Thank you," I say, heat rising in my cheeks.

There is an awkward silence that feels heavy with expectation, and I shy away. Sensing my discomfort, Sophia's tone changes and she becomes playful once more, "Don't go getting all big-headed on me now. Any more than you already are!"

"Big-headed? How so?" I ask, amused.

We are back to laughing now. We roll about on the floor in tandem as Sophia rehashes her first opinion of me. Apparently, the reason people don't warm to me is that I carry myself with a sense of superiority.

"Really? And I thought I did a good job of hiding it," I joke.

Sophia asks me in a more serious tone now, why I volunteered to help her, on her first day at school. This is dangerous territory. If I share too much, I could freak her out. If I don't share enough, I may never get this moment again.

"You reminded me of me. I've never fit in. Quite frankly, I think I've never wanted to. When I saw you sat nervously at your desk, I felt an instant connection. You were an outsider too. Selfishly, I knew that you wouldn't be for long."

"What do you mean?"

"A girl like you. You can be anyone you want to be. You'd have been snapped up fast by anyone in the school once you'd found your feet. I knew after a day, you'd never even consider being my friend."

Sophia placed her hand on mine as she spoke, "Then you don't know me as well as you think you do."

I sit up straighter and clear my throat.

"Have you ever had a girlfriend?" Sophia suddenly queries.

"No. Never," I say, shaking my head.

"You ever had a boyfriend?"

"No."

The response surprises me. Sophia is stunning. How on earth has she remained single her whole life?

She hesitates, "I struggle to...trust people."

Knowing what I do about her father, this makes complete sense. I instantly feel guilty. She thinks she can trust me, the version of me she sees. How could I have ever let this go this far?

"Lucas, can I try something?"

The light outside has dimmed, and her room is caught between light and darkness.

"Yes, of course," is my response, perplexed by what she wants to do.

Sophia edges forward along the floor. Her face so close I can feel her breath against my skin and see the splashes of russet and tan along her irises. Gently, she wipes away the curling hair that dangles in front of my eyes. My body feels so alive, almost electric. The pull I feel towards her is overwhelming, but I remain still and longing. Sophia's lips touch mine at last. At first, the kiss is soft and mild. Neither of us moving. Then, I find myself inching myself ever closer and holding my hand against the back of her head. Intertwining my fingers with her soft hair. She pushes open my mouth and finds my tongue. I can taste the sweetness of sherbet as we move against one another. The feeling is better than anything I've felt before. When we ultimately part, we are breathless. I keep her close to me, foreheads touching, and I immediately want to kiss her again. To never stop kissing her.

"That was my first kiss," I whisper.

"Mine too," Sophia replies, still inches away from my mouth.

Fred's face comes to my mind's eye and spoils the moment. Now more than ever, I long to keep her safe from him. By now, Janice has left for work, and I hear the buzz of the TV downstairs where Fred watches sitcoms. Reluctantly, I excuse myself to go to the bathroom, ensuring I close Sophia's bedroom door on my way out.

The note is already written in my pocket. When thinking about what I could do to stop Fred's antics, I thought of what would stop me. What we have in common is anonymity. It is the foundation of our acts. Without it, everything crumbles. Inscribed on the letter reads, 'I know what you do to Sophia.' Short and to the point. I place it on Fred and Janice's bed, knowing he will find it before she comes back from work. To ensure Sophia doesn't suspect anything is amiss, I go to the toilet. By the time I make it back onto the landing, Fred is stood in my way.

"It is getting late, I think it is time for you to wrap things up," he announces with eyes unblinking and bold.

I rush into Sophia's room to gather my things before he finds the note while I am there. After saying my goodbyes, I feel the need to kiss Sophia once more. Fred hovers nearby, making this impossible. All I can do is squeeze her hand as I walk towards the front door. It closes behind me with Fred's forceful hand. Heading back home, I am filled with so many conflicting emotions. The effervescent joy of my first kiss, and the fear that Fred won't go to his bedroom before going to Sophia's.

Chapter Ten

I wake to the sound of bird's tweeting outside, and the sun beaming through my window. Last night I slept the whole night. I can't deny how refreshed and restored I feel – coupled with the euphoria of what happened between Sophia and me. Caught up in my emotions, I almost forget the alarming reality. Did my note work? It is Saturday and without the common ground of school, I hope Sophia is available to meet up. I'm sure, by her demeanour alone, I can gather a sense of how things went.

I bolt out of bed and head for the shower. The warm water pours over me, unveiling my sensuality. As I rub my hands over my skin, I imagine they are Sophia's hands. I've never felt more like a teenage boy. Here I am, daydreaming about a girl. The thought of her lips is enough to send me over the edge.

Leaving the confines of the shower cubicle, I notice how the bathroom has filled with foggy steam. The mirror screeches as I wipe away the moisture. I stand naked and dripping with my wet hair pushed back off my face, wondering if Sophia is doing the same thing just meters away. My body no longer feels like my own. I feel part of me is still pressed up against Sophia, parting her lips. As my fingers explore my desires, a knock bangs against the door, bringing me back to Earth.

"Lucas! You've been in there ages; I need a shower too."

I quickly wrap a towel around my waist and head to my room to get ready.

"All yours mum," I call back.

Inside my room, I marvel at the sight beyond my window. Sophia, walking steadfast towards my house. Clothing flings into the air chaotically as I search for something to wear. I step hurriedly into a pair of jeans and shove on a white tee. The doorbell sings as I fasten the last button.

"Coming!" I shout, bounding down the stairs.

Keenly, I open the front door and bask in all her glory. A smile takes over her face, so wide that new dimples form around her cheeks.

"Hi."

"Hi," she speaks happily.

"So... what are you up to today?"

"I was hoping we could hang out if you don't have any other plans?"

We discuss where we could go and settle on Folsom Lake. It is a bit of a walk unless we can catch a ride. I enquire with my parents and practically jump for joy when my dad offers to give us a lift. We make our way out to the car together, taking in the beauty of the day.

"Looks like the suns coming out. Do you mind if I put down the windows?" my dad asks, and we comply.

The weather plants a seed, and I stop dead in my tracks.

"Hang on, let me just grab something real quick," I call out before rushing back into the house. My hand grabs the camera on my desk, and I pull the strap over my head, allowing it to dangle with ease.

He sets off with the roar of the engine and we sit idly next to one another. In the rush of air, Sophia's hair whips around her head, momentarily covering her almond eyes from me. I notice her hand laying against the seat and consider taking it in mine. I flash my eyes at the rear-view mirror assessing my dad's attention. He remains fixed onto the road, so I act on my instinct. As we both gaze out at the passing scenery, I find her hand and push my fingers between hers. Without looking back, I feel for her acceptance. She squeezes back, and I grin with both delight and embarrassment – not yet used to this otherworldly feeling. The haze of brick finally replaces with forest green trees. As we park up, the expansive, shimmering lake comes into view.

"It's lovely," Sophia enthuses.

"Enjoy your day folks. I'll come back for you both in a couple of hours."

Pebbles crunch under the car wheels as my dad drives away, leaving us to ponder over the beautiful scenery. The air feels so fresh and inviting. Sophia lets go of my hand and begins to prance around the place, twirling like a ballerina.

"I love it here! I feel so free."

Crossing my arms, I just watch and take her in. She looks completely at ease. All indications so far point to my note fulfilling my intention. The moment is too irresistible. I take my canon between my fingers and allow the lens to grind into focus. The camera shutters click and churn, capturing Sophia mid-spin, hair floating with rapture. Before she could stop, I zoom in and snap a shot of her perfect face up-close. She subsequently protests, so I let go of the camera and pull her gently onto the path, eager to start our adventure. We glide, hand in hand, around the lake, watching as the light sparkles against the surface. Folsom lies northwest of Sacramento within the hills of El Dorado. The area is synonymous with outdoor sports. Out here, you can do everything from camping to water-skiing. Dotted along the sandy beach, early risers relax and enjoy the boats peppering the reservoir. I search for a spot to soak up the sights. Eventually, we reach a worn bench and rest.

"I don't want this day to end," she utters, glancing out across the dam.

"That is how I felt yesterday."

Sophia turns to me and plants a light kiss against my cheek.

"How did you sleep?" I enquire, searching her expression for any sign of change.

"I had the best sleep. Probably the best I've had since moving here."

Relief floods from my pores. My letter did work. Thank goodness. The conversation switches to how I know about Folsom. I tell her about the many family trips I've had out here and the time I pushed my sister into the lake – much to her annoyance. On another occasion, I was almost bitten by a rattlesnake. They aren't all that uncommon round here.

Sophia unpacks more about her life and explains how she's always wanted a big brother, someone to look after her and someone to look up to. We search the sky for shapes among the clouds and stop occasionally to make out. Lingering between kisses, our eyes meet.

"Were you ever afraid that you would never find this?" Sophia nods towards our close bodies.

"Yes," I lie, I never even contemplated about love. I didn't understand it and wasn't sure if I was even capable of it. Of course, now I know better, "you?"

Her eyes drop to her fingers, and I see her cuticles are bitten back, red and raw. As her hands move, I catch a glimpse of her arm. A long, deep and angry scar protrudes from her skin. It causes my jaw to drop and a gasp to escape from my throat. Seeing my reaction, she immediately tugs her sleeve down.

"I've been afraid of a lot of things. I'm just glad that I met you when I did."

I do not speak to this, just wrap my arm around her shoulders as worry sets in. As well as her father, Sophia is a threat to herself. I need to know she's okay, even when I'm not there. What if Fred starts up again? What if Sophia does something stupid?

I'd made a promise to myself after kissing Sophia. I would no longer violate her trust. However, I know now that I must. One more time. A plan morphs into my mind. As night falls and Sophia sleeps, I will find somewhere unsuspecting to place a camera. A camera I can control. A camera where I can always be with Sophia.

Chapter Eleven

Things feel different. I'm off my game. The dark deeds I once yearned for would excite me to my very core. After years of perfecting my craft, I felt confident about my endeavours. Assured. Tonight, the key glistens in my hand and I find myself hesitating. A frost has descended across the ground, casting an icy glaze over the surfaces. My black canvas smeared with white. The key's edges graze against my skin as they turn over in my palm. I think back to the first time I stood here and the motivations that drove me. How different I am now.

The key glides into the lock. A swell of adrenaline builds in my chest. I fight against its pleasure. This mission is not for me, it is for her. The door swings open, releasing the familiar smell that infuses Sophia's clothes. Closing the door behind me, the usual darkness persists all around. The quietness envelops like a heavy duvet. With my eyes adjusting, silhouettes of the house begin to slowly develop - just as polaroids do. Out of the corner of my eye, I spot a shape that is not in keeping with the lounge. A shadow within the shadows. Before I could escape, the figure begins to speak.

"I was hoping you'd return," Fred declares.

Fear paralyses my limbs. My feet anchor to the ground, unable to work.

"It took me a while to figure it out. Not the note. I knew that was you straight away. What I couldn't understand was how you knew."

The words cascade from his mouth with such arrogance, I knew that he'd manage to answer his dilemma.

"Sophia would never tell anyone, she has too much at stake. Of course, it didn't stop me from asking her, just to be sure. There's no disguising true disbelief. She seemed as shocked as me when I showed her the note."

My fists clench at this information. No. What has he told her? I think back to the perfect day I've shared with Sophia. Had he spoken to her before or after? It didn't make sense why she'd act so happy if she knew what I'd done.

"The only possible explanation is that you somehow saw something for yourself, so I asked her. Did you ever give Lucas a key? Well, she seemed to piece things together pretty quickly herself after I said that."

A vision replays in my head. Me scooping up the keys from the pavement, Sophia confused from the silence of their descent.

"I have to applaud you really. Innocently dropping the key on the concrete, why would anyone think that suspicious?" A laugh ripples through his chest, he's amused. "I have to ask Lucas, exactly how many times have you broken into my house?"

A thought suddenly dawns on me. Where is everyone? How is he managing to speak so candidly?

"Where is Sophia?" I muster.

An even louder and more sinister cackle rips through the air. To him, I am a fox caught in a snare.

"They aren't here, Lucas. I arranged for them to go on a last-minute spa break. I thought it would be more fun this way."

"What would be more fun?" I ask, petrified by his response.

Fred's dark outline stands tall and creeps towards me. His black eyes move so close to mine, I can see their unblinking dominance. If I die here, Sophia will never know the truth. I will never be able to protect her. As Fred's immense body towers over me, a fight or flight response takes over. I raise my hand, still grasping the key, and pierce it against Fred's neck. As he fumbles against the wound, wincing in pain, I fling open the door and make a run for it. I am dumbfounded when I hear Fred's cries turn to laughter yet again. What could he possibly find funny now? He stands, with blood dripping down him, looking at me. Unflinching. He isn't coming after me and he isn't calling for an ambulance. What I can't see is what he is truly starring at. Unlike Fred, I don't notice my downstairs light turn on and my parents approach the door. The seal respires behind me when they open up onto the scene. I spin around to face them, and it is only then that I notice the blood on my hands.

Chapter Twelve

After the onslaught of screams subsides, the interrogation starts.

"What the hell is going on?" my father shrieks as my mum rushes over to Fred, now collapsed against the stone drenched with red.

I pull at her clothes, begging her to leave him alone. Neighbours stand alarmed near their doorways, unable to turn themselves away from the drama unfolding before them. Some manage to rush back into their homes, probably to call for the police.

My trainers drag along the floor as I yell, "Stop, please, mum, listen to me! He was going to kill me!"

At this, she finally heels. Her wide, glossy eyes shift from Fred to me and then back again.

"What do you mean?"

"I was in Fred's house and – "

"Why were you in his house, Lucas?" my father snaps.

"I...I..."

"Lucas?"

As I stand floundering for words, a way to explain all of this without sounding crazy, sirens ricochet from afar. Neighbours now encircle us, asking if everything is alright. If they can help.

I watch as my mum presses against Fred's neck, leaving me to shake in the shadows.

The sirens call, now ear-splittingly loud, couples with the flashing of blue lights. An assault on the senses. A cop car tails behind the ambulance which brakes next to the scene. Out disperse medics that hurry to the causality. The police loiter more measured in the background, taking in the picture.

"What happened?" a paramedic asks while the other presses a bandage firmly against Fred's injury. Blood seeps through almost instantaneously. His face now drained of colour.

Fred's trembling finger rises in the air. Everyone turns to follow its direction. He is pointing at me. I back away into the road repeating, "He hurt her, he hurt her."

My body connects with something, and I spin round to see the two officers, solemn and serious.

"Who hurt her? Why not sit down and tell us all about it."

My parents, privy to the moment, scurry towards my side. The second officer, a female, taller than the male officer, takes me by the arm towards the curb. She asks after my name and proceeds to make a note of it in her pad. She enquires over my age, and I inform her that I am fifteen years old, and they glance at one another.

"What happened tonight?" the male officer asks cautiously.

I wipe my quivering hands over my face, forgetting that they are dried with blood. As I look up, I see how frightened my mum is. Tears burn in my throat, aching to be set free. I swallow hard and find my voice.

"Fred raped Sophia."

My mum immediately clasps her mouth with both hands.

"Who is Sophia?" an officer raises, not yet aware of the sickening circumstance.

My father clarifies before I can, "His daughter."

They were not expecting this by the shuffle in their stance. The atmosphere tenses and my parent's rigid exterior seems to melt, just a little. Shock morphing into fury. My mum tells them that Fred and his family only moved in across the road a few weeks ago. One of the officer's leave, likely to check the premises for any further causalities or to interview further witnesses.

"When did this happen?" the remaining officer questions.

I cannot quell the images as they surface. His feet. The shrill of the mattress. Her pyjamas abandoned on the floor. Her rasping cries.

"A couple of nights ago."

"How did Fred become hurt, Lucas?"

My tears bubble over, unable to remain contained. Finally, my father's arm hugs against me as I respond, "I did it. I hurt him, okay? I was afraid for my life."

"Why were you afraid?"

"Because... because he found out that I knew what he'd been doing, and I was trying to stop him."

"You've done a great job of cooperating, Lucas. We are going to need to take you down to the station now. Do you understand?"

I nod, the severity of the situation weighing heavily on my shoulders. As my mum and dad start to cry, the officer arrests me and declares my rights. As the crowds look on, I am taken into the back of the police car. To them, I am the bad guy here.

Silence suffuses as the door shuts behind me. Brief relief from the carnage. For the entire ride, all I can do is stifle my emotions and push back against the hope that lingers at the back of my mind. The hope that Fred dies.

The station smells of sweat and shoe polish. The female officer speaks with her colleagues and returns to my side. She tells me that the following procedure is to photograph my body for any potential evidence. I am led into a small, dense room where I am told to stand still against the white wall. Another officer, this time burly with muscle, takes over the commands.

"Spread your hands."

The camera in his hand fixates on my own. The familiar snap of the lens proceeds. He asks me to turn them over, palms up. I follow his instructions without comment.

"Look straight ahead for me."

Flashes blur out my vision as he takes photographs of my face. Next, are my clothes and shoes. My eyes follow his gaze, as he zooms in on any stray speckles of blood. Afterwards, he passes me a clear, plastic bag. Unsure of the reason, I scowl at the officer.

"Strip. The bag is for your clothing."

Timidly, I peel off my top and jeans, placing each one into the bag provided. I stand, cold and afraid, facing the glaring interior.

"Socks and underwear too."

Our eyes meet and he simply nods. I abide grudgingly, trying my best to hide what is left of my modesty. They search my skin for any marks or blood to photograph. With that, the female officer provides me with a change of clothes and leads me to a custody cell.

"Where are my parents?" I panic.

"They are on their way. As a minor, they will be present during our questioning later. Until then, you will wait in here."

Her hand gestures to the inside of the confinement. I step inside and scan my surroundings. The windowless room is absent of colour or furniture. Jutting out from the back wall is some kind of bed, topped with a thin cushion. A grey toilet and basin are the only remaining features in the space. As the door slams shut, I realise how bright the fluorescent lights gleam. Yet there is nowhere to take shelter. Nowhere to hide. With nothing to do but wait, my body gravitates towards the bed. As I rock back and forth, unsure of my future and the story I will tell, I spot a security camera watching me from the ceiling. How the tables have turned.

Chapter Thirteen

"The charges are serious, Lucas - aggravated assault, breaking and entering. You are lucky Mr Andrews is still alive. If you have anything to tell us that may help your case, now is the time to say."

When I don't respond, the Investigating Officer shrugs at my dad, the only parent in the room. My mum was too upset to attend.

Sensing my anxiety, my dad presses the police, "Shouldn't we wait until council arrives?"

"Mr Stevenson, we aren't trying to trick you into anything here. You've already admitted that you stabbed –"

"I don't think stabbed is the right turn of phrase," my dad scoffs.

"Lucas punctured the main artery in Mr Andrews' neck. He could have died."

The atmosphere fills with silence. No one is talking about the elephant in the room. The reason why I hurt Fred. How much admission of guilt do I want to display? With every word, I could be increasing my sentence. I glance at my dad, gleaning for moral support. He nods – just.

"As I said, Fred raped Sophia."

Both officers remain sat, unfazed by my statement. The female, who has been fairly quiet so far, turns her posture to be more directly aligned with mine. Noticing how she has captured my attention; she takes over the conversation.

"Lucas, take us back, please. We need to know how this event took place. Without an account, the allegation means nothing."

A sigh reverberates across my chest, and I consider my options. Do I tell the truth or a version of the truth that hides my own transgressions? Picking at my fleshy cuticles, my mind flashes to Sophia and our day out yesterday. Her arm. Her scar. I don't want to cause her any more pain.

"I was worried about her, she seemed scared sometimes. Whenever I brought up Richmond, she'd just shut down, like the memory was too painful or something. So, I started watching over her."

"Watching over how?"

"I made a copy of Sophia's key."

The room feels almost padded. Soundproof. In this small chamber, words settle with such clarity. My dad glares at me, astounded. Have I said too much?

"I know how that sounds, I really do, but I just knew something dodgy was going off in that house and then when I let myself in – I didn't break in – I just opened the door as any regular person would, I just sat and watched her, looked through her things. You know, for clues."

The words are falling from my lips like vomit. Spoken aloud, they sound ludicrous, even for my standards. The officer's expression affirms as much. Changing tact, the male officer offers me some encouragement.

"Okay, so you are in Sophia's room. Then what?"

"I hear Fred get up, he makes his way to her bedroom door, so I hide – under the bed. That's when it happens. Fred comes in, doesn't say a word. At first, I think he's caught me but after a few seconds I hear him climb into Sophia's bed and things start to happen."

"What things, Lucas?"

"Do I really need to say?"

He nods his head and speaks categorically, "Yes, we need to know exactly what happened."

"Sophia's pyjamas come off and land on the floor next to me. Then...then...the mattress starts to move, and I can hear Fred... grunting," I can hardly contain myself now, my voice breaks as I revisit the memory, "When he is finished, he leaves, and I hear Sophia crying."

I tell them how I did nothing, said nothing, fearing Sophia's reaction. They ask me about the next day and if Sophia ever told me outright what was going on. She never did. We discuss everything right up to the evening I let myself into Fred's house. I explain how sinister he was, how threatening he came across. They probe further, unsatisfied with my account.

"What made you feel like your life was in danger? Did Mr Andrews have a weapon at all?"

"No, he didn't, but he told me that he had sent Sophia and Janice away so that he wouldn't be disturbed. The anger in his face - I read between the lines. I panicked."

Nobody speaks for some time. My dad's hand squeezes my leg comfortingly. Everything is out in the open now, and it is true what they say, I feel lighter for it. The female officer leans across the table with searching eyes. I think she might take my hands in hers and tell me how brave I was for sticking up for

Sophia. How lucky it was that I discovered such horrific things were taking place.

"Lucas," the tone she speaks, deftly serious, immediately worries me, "the problem is, we spoke with Sophia. She says that her father never hurt her - that the rape never happened."

Everything in the room begins to spin, a vortex of colours and light. Underfoot, the floor turns to quicksand. I am falling, waiting for my body to smack the linoleum and orientate me back into reality. My father is speaking but it sounds muffled like he is underwater. Tremors radiate across my core as I close my eyes and try to steady myself. Slowly, the tilt of my vision realigns, and my senses attune themselves once more.

Now cemented on my chair, I announce to the room calmly, "I won't answer any more of your questions without my lawyer present."

Chapter Fourteen

My attorney, Bob Mathews, underdoes his jacket button to free his bulging belly as he sits across from me. Under his glasses, his hooded eyes twitch. I can't decide if it is an involuntary habit like Tourettes or if he's just tired. Either way, you can tell that he's been a public defender for most of his life and has lost some of his lustre for it.

As I rehash the events leading up to my arrest, he leans absently back on his chair, causing the fabric along his shirt to stretch and reveal pockets of body hair. When I pause, he doesn't interject. It is hard to know when to stop talking. The effect causes me to divulge even more than I did with the police. As I reach the bloody climax of last night, he creaks forward in his chair, takes off his glasses and wipes his eyes with his large, bulbous hands.

My dad chirps up before I can get a word in, "So how bad is it?"

"The problem is Lucas's account does not marry up with Sophia's statement. Lucas has already confessed to unlawful entry and assault. Fortunately, we aren't looking at attempted murder."

"But I didn't intend to kill anyone!" I object.

"I know that, but under the circumstances, they could argue as such."

"Then why aren't they?"

"I guess that the police are working on other charges - charges they have a better chance of gaining a conviction with."

"Such as?" my dad barks.

"Well, stalking for one."

I can't believe my ears. Sophia and I are friends, more than that. People at school can testify to that. As soon as the thought enters my mind, I remember who I am. Of course, no one would care enough about me to do that. It is my word against Sophia's.

"Lucas and Sophia are friends," my father announces, responding to my internal struggles.

"Do friends spy on each other? The court could twist everything Lucas did to show that he manipulated her into forming a friendship, but his real motivations were predatory."

The portrait he paints is so accurate, why would anyone side with someone like me? Deep down I always knew what I was doing was wrong, but never did I intend to physically hurt someone. I am obsessed with Sophia and obsession can be misconstrued so easily. A headache rages in my frontal lobe. I thought my feelings for Sophia were mutual.

"Why would she lie?" I enquire openly, "This all makes no sense. Sophia and I were becoming so close. She wouldn't pull a stunt like this unless she had a good reason to."

Mr Mathews exhales with a sigh and scratches his receding hairline.

"I'm no psychologist but Stockholm syndrome comes to mind. Could be an angle for us. The only problem is, we'd need to prove that the abuse has been going on for years. Fred has no priors and Janice is standing by him."

"If I could just talk to Sophia myself, find out what she is so afraid of, I know I'd be able to get her to admit the truth."

"I won't lie, Sophia changing her story is our best solution here. We could negotiate your charges, since you've already pleaded guilty, and we could even mitigate the need to go to trial."

Doing so lawfully is out of the question according to Mr Mathews. My only glimmer of hope at the moment is that he is certain that I'll make bail. Like Fred, my record is clean (on paper at least), and so Bob says, my youth will also work in my favour.

Mr Mathews leaves the room to file the paperwork for my bond. It gives me some alone time with my dad. I need to ask him to do me a favour. I have a feeling the room is being recorded, but the reward outweighs the risk.

"Dad, I need you to speak to Sophia, find out what is going on. You know everything now – all of it. Ask her to show you her sketchbook. You'll see, she feels the same way about me that I feel about her."

My dad takes me in his arms and tells me he will do his best. As he pulls away, still inches close, he asks if there is anything that might prove my version of events. My mind whirls as I fight against the throbbing pain.

After several seconds I reply, "Ask her about Richmond, something happened there, I just know it."

The click of the door interrupts our conversation and in steps a police officer eager to return me to my cell. My time is up.

As they lead me from the room, I call back to my dad, "Tell mum that I'm doing fine, okay?"

He nods without answering, coughing back tears. I've never needed my dad more. My entire destiny rests with him, and there is no way of knowing if he'll succeed.

Chapter Fifteen

Sophia

The water isn't hot enough. I need it to scorch my skin clean. To take my mind away from the predicament that I find myself in. The mess that I've pulled Lucas into. Of course, I feel guilty. I've walked around carrying guilt on my back for years. You could say I'm a pro at it, but I don't feel like a champion. I was stupid to think that Sacramento would fix things. Just thinking about my dad makes me want to rip the flesh from my bones. And Lucas knew.

When I saw the note, it was the first time that I'd seen his delicate, cursive handwriting. Really seen it I mean. The words, his words, were trying to protect me. I wish that he'd come to me first.

What a stupid, brilliant boy. To imagine him now, watching me, without me knowing, pulls my heart in two. On the one hand, he is just another person using me for his own pleasure. On the other hand, the very idea of it exhilarates my senses. Does that make me as twisted as him? In reality, I'm much, much worse. Lucas risked his own life to save my own, yet I may as well have thrown him to the lions.

Lucas thinks that I am soft and gentle and sincere. That is how I want him to think of me. If he knew what I really am, he'd never look at me the same way again.

A knock vibrates through the house, stalling my thoughts. I launch out of the bath, water spraying everywhere, and wrap a towel around me. The bangs become more urgent as I make my way to my room. Peering out of my bedroom window, I see who is at the door. It is Lucas's dad, Mr Stevenson. He sees me with desperate eyes. I shake my head, knowing what is about to come. My mum barges out of the house and practically lunges at him. As I crack my window open further, I hear her telling him to leave our family alone. The wetness pooling in my eyes finally tips over. So much injustice. The door slams on her way back into the house. A force so large it jolts my tears away. She stampedes up the stairs to find me propped up against the wall.

"Sophia, get away from the window. You are not to speak with that man, do you hear me?" she yells.

I nod silently. I am tired of talking to her, of lying to her. She swoops in and closes my curtains.

"Try and get some sleep."

It is 7 pm. I do not want to sleep. Instead, I twitch open the curtains and stare towards Lucas's house. Gazing back at me stands Mr Stevenson, yet to renter his property. He is mouthing something that I can't make out. Gently, I ease the window open fully to get a better listen.

"Tonight," he says while pointing to his front door. "Tonight."

It takes me a few moments before the penny drops. To let him know that I understand, I smile and tap on my wrist. He lifts both hands and shows me ten fingers and then he flashes two more – midnight. I show him a thumbs up, signalling that I know exactly what he wants me to do.

I don't know how Lucas does this. I'm struggling to steady my breathing. Even though I know that Mr Stevenson awaits my arrival across the road, my body won't cooperate. I need to control myself. I close my eyes and recite words of comfort; my dad is not here. I am safe. I will not get caught. I will not screw this up like I have screwed up so many other things in my life. My fingernails dig into the palms of my clenched fists, frustration building.

All I need to do is get out of the front door. Simple. My key feels heavy in my pocket. It has somehow doubled in weight due to the focus it holds over my mind. I glance at my mum's bedroom. Her door is shut. She sleeps soundly. My pupils dilate, allowing me to see my environment better. As softly as I can, I tip-toe across the landing and begin my descent downstairs. Every movement plays out as if in slow motion. I don't want to make a single mistake, yet as soon as I press my heel against the step halfway down, a creak escapes from the wooden slats. Flinching, I cease motion and listen intently. Only when I am content that my mum remains aloof do I continue my journey. My reverse Mount Everest. The front door is so close yet so far. It practically beams in front of me, calling me closer. With my feet finally on solid ground, I survey my surroundings. This is where it happened. Where my dad and Lucas confronted one another. Where everything unravelled.

My mouth feels parched. I can't waste any more time. My hand twists the key in the lock. I take my time, ensuring the click is as quiet as possible. My sweaty palm rests against the back of the door as I start to ease it open. Cold air hisses inside, nipping at my fingers like invisible claws. I step out, joining the night, and close the door behind me. Everything is so still and silent. Nothing but the moon and the stars look overhead as I creep across the street towards Lucas's house.

Mr Stevenson smiles at me from the dining room window as I approach. I try the handle of the door and smile when it gives way, allowing me to enter inside.

"We have to whisper," he announces, pointing to the ceiling above. "How have you been?"

I can't sustain eye contact with this question hanging between us. Such a simple question with so many possible answers.

"How is Lucas?" I deflect.

This time, it is Mr Stevenson that turns away. He begins to rock back and forth on the balls of his feet, hands stuffed into pockets.

"He's in big trouble, Sophia, big trouble no thanks to you."

Even though I expected as much, the reality is hard to swallow.

"I'm so sorry," is all I can manage to say.

"Why lie? Why are you protecting your father?"

I shake my head furiously, "You've got it all wrong. I'm not protecting him, I'm protecting myself."

A car drives past outside, illuminating the street outside. I automatically jump in response, my body on edge to the possibility of anyone else listening in.

"Lucas told me to ask you, what happened in Richmond?"

My heart practically skips a beat in my chest. A torrent of images flashes before me; a drunken haze, a dark road, and a bump in the night no one saw coming. Least of all me.

Chapter Sixteen

Mr Stevenson guides me to sit on one of his armchairs. My automatic response is to flinch and turn away, but I somehow manage to overcome my defence mechanism and sit onto the edge of the patterned seat. It is only when I taste the coppery blood in my mouth that I realise I've been biting my cuticles. The only way I can stop myself from gnawing at my skin is to clutch the cushion underneath me. I grip as if I am holding on for dear life. In a way I am.

"I was fourteen when it happened," I began.

"The abuse?" Mr Stevenson asks, and I shake my head.

"I was a walking cliché. My parents were constantly fighting and all that did was drive me away from home. I'd fallen into the wrong crowd. It wasn't long before I started drinking and smoking pot." I take a deep inhale before continuing, unable to gauge Mr Stevenson's reaction. "The gang that I was involved with enjoyed joy riding. It was the one thing that petrified me. Over time, the more I drank and smoked, the less I cared. Then the day came when they asked me to steal a car. I didn't know what to do," Mr Stevenson sighs, and I feel the need to expand, "I know it sounds stupid, but I thought that the only way we'd stay friends is if I did everything that they asked."

"If they were real friends, Sophia they wouldn't have asked you to break the law."

"I was a rebellious teenager. I just wanted to be liked," as I speak, I can hear the defensive tone in my voice and quickly remember the point of this conversation. "In the end, I decided to take my dad's car and pretend that I had stolen it. They were so... impressed."

"I'm guessing your dad found out?"

My fingers dig hard into the cushion creating a crunching sound.

"We'd spent the evening getting drunk and high. I was cruising down this low-lit highway. I can still hear the music blaring. The road was so quiet, it was like no one else was out that night, just us. All it took was one second of me turning to talk to my friends in the back seat. I heard the impact before I felt it," my eyes tighten unconsciously as I talk, the repressed memory alive once again. The sound of blaring music is now replaced with the screeching of tires. "The thud was so forceful we were thrown forwards, yet no one said a word. We just stared at one another with sheer terror. I didn't dare look."

"So you just drove off? Without checking?"

I hang my head in shame and watch as tears splatter onto the floor.

"How does this have anything to do with Lucas?" Mr Stevenson retorts.

"When I returned the car, the bonnet was all concaved and there was... blood. Whatever happened, I knew it was bad, but when my dad saw it he didn't flip out like I expected him to. He calmly asked what route I'd driven and said that he'd sort it. My dad left the house that morning and didn't come home until hours later. When he did, he had a brand-new car," I pause briefly afraid to finish my story. To admit the things that followed. Things far worse than the car crash. "He drove me out into the middle of nowhere. I noticed soil under his fingernails as he held the steering wheel. When he finally parked up, we were facing a mound of freshly dug dirt. He didn't have to tell me what he had done. I already knew. We just sat gazing out at the grave before us in silence. His hand resting on my thigh. He told me that he'd always protect me, that he'd never share my secret… if I did a favour for him too."

Mr Stevenson doesn't ask for me to explain more than I already have. I know from the sadness in his eyes that he understands. I watch through blurry vision as his sadness morphs into despair, realising what this means for his son.

"You see, if I speak out so will he. I'm so sorry," I sob uncontrollably.

I can't bear to see Mr Stevenson's sorrow any longer. I unclench my hands from the rim of the armchair and feel as they ache slowly into a straight position. As I stand, I am suddenly aware of the snot that has formed above my top lip. Embarrassed, I wipe it with the top of my sleeve and then turn to leave.

"Sophia, wait."

I hover at the front door, facing away from Lucas's father. Away from my responsibilities. There is nothing that I can do to fix Lucas's problems. Neither of us can be saved. Before Mr Stevenson can say another word, I open the door and step back into the dark.

Chapter Seventeen

"You'll get used to it," Bob Mathews declares as the officer attaches the location tag around my ankle.

The strap clicks tight against my skin. I scratch at the surrounding area with a frown. I am only permitted to leave my house during the hours between eight am and eight pm. Under no circumstances am I to enter Sophia's house, regardless of the time.

"It is only until your court hearing in a couple of weeks," Mathews elaborates.

The device isn't as heavy as it looks but is uncomfortable nether-the-less. A constant reminder of my impending persecution.

"Can I shower with it?" I question.

"For up to an hour. Everything else you need to know is detailed in this pamphlet."

Mr Mathews passes me a small leaflet on all the things that I can and can't do while out on bail. I notice the section outlining the consequences for rule-breaking.

I point my finger against the red text, "It says here that the police will be immediately notified if I do something wrong. Would that affect my bail? Or is it like three strikes and you're out?"

The smirk on my face quickly subsides when taking in Mr Mathews' stern glare. Blatantly, this isn't a good time to be cracking jokes.

"Lucas, you would be straight back here, and it would not paint your character in a good light," he insists with a serious expression, "so don't get any ideas."

The officers reunite me with the clothes that I arrived in and lead me to a policeman standing stoic behind a computer. He checks that I understand all the restrictions within my bail, and I say that I do, although I haven't been given enough time to peruse the leaflet clutched in my left hand. He informs me that the consequences of such actions would result in me forfeiting my bail rights, just as Mr Mathews advised. Beggars can't be chooses as the saying goes. Cell life ceased my night-time hobbies, so I guess I've had plenty of time to prepare for such a morbid existence.

As I am taken to the exit of the station, I make out my parents with arms outstretched, hellbent on taking me home. I run to them and inhale the familiar scent etched into their skin and clothes. The warm sun drenches us in natural light as we leave, arm in arm. My body aches with relief. I surrender to the feeling, practically glowing from cheek to cheek, until my father intercepts the moment with a statement that stops me in my tracks.

"I spoke with Sophia," he whispers against my ear, "and you were right about Richmond."

I snap my head towards his face, eager to hear more.

"Later."

For the whole car ride home my mind whirls with the possibilities of their discussion. I am so in my own head that all

I can do is nod as my mother's consistent statements until the car eventually comes to a stop. My thoughts momentarily shift from my father's revelations to the prospect of walking into my house for the first time in weeks. The very building I had been craving during my time inside now stands proudly before me in all its glory. My feet shuffle inside with the same care and consideration of my night stalks. For this is a precious, delicate moment that should be savoured. I walk upstairs like Bambi taking his first steps. The expanse of my house feels infinite after the confines of prison life.

Desperate for some sentiment of comfort, I decide to put off speaking with my father and try to enjoy my first night of freedom. I take a long, hot shower for one hour exactly and fall into bed, ready to sleep for as many hours as my mind would allow. Consciously, my mind does not allow me to fully unwind. Minutes in, I dream of being locked inside a coffin, buried alive. Fear races through my veins as I bang against the wooden lid. Nothing but dust escapes. No one hears my cries. When I wake, bolt upright in bed, I can sense the dampness of my sheets. Panic triggering perspiration. Slowly, I regain a steady rhythm with my breath and peel myself from my bed. Searching for something concrete and real, my fingertips sweep around the walls of my room. Walls not much larger than my cell. I am still trapped. My freedom is constricted and limited by time.

Time.

I search for the clock on my wall and through the cracks of light breaking through my curtains I can just make out the late hour. It stirs something deep within me. A yearning. I gradually pull back the fabric and open up onto the world outside. A quiet haven empty of people and problems. It feels like greeting an old friend. A friend I'd all but lost touch with, but despite the distance, they still welcome you with open arms.

Something catches my eye or my heart. I can feel her presence beyond the wall. Beyond my reach. As I scan the streets, I see what my senses already know. Sophia. She stands in my mirror image, in front of her window, her own shard of impenetrable glass. Watching me, watching her. I step closer and press my body against the pane. Just like all those months ago when we laughed in the tall grass, finding shapes amongst the clouds, our hands outstretch but this time they do not meet. We both push our palms against the glass and feel for the electricity. Her eyes fix on mine and her mouth parts open, but she does not speak. I see her breath mist against the window, her panting rasps igniting my own. Her fingers glide against the softness of her blouse. I watch in awe as she pulls at her buttons. Eyes never leaving my face. I cannot turn away. Her bewitching glare intensifies as she slides the top from her skin. She pushes at her waist, dropping her skirt to the floor. I follow her lines and pour over her every curve. Heat rises from my body as I yearn to turn sight into touch. Instinctively, I tear at my clothing until they are nothing but a heap on the carpet. We stand naked and absorb one another without judgement, without fear. I long for her embrace, for her sweet lips. It is only now that I set my gaze on the ground. For it is those same lips that keep me locked in my house. It is her silence that threatens to send me to prison and keep me from being with her ever again. When I lift my head to resume our stance, she is already gone, lost within the shadows. I guess it is up to me to drag her into the light.

Chapter Eighteen

"Lucas, wake up, Lucas."

I wake to see my father peering over me from my bedside, already dressed. It takes me a second to remember where I am.

"What's going on?"

"Let's take a drive. Be ready to leave in ten."

The urgency in his voice propels me upright. I stretch my arms and arch my back before throwing the covers off my body. How can I ache? It is as if my body needs to reaccustom to a proper mattress. Leaving the duvet unmade, I decide to throw on a pair of dark blue denim jeans and a polo shirt. I'd almost forgotten the heavenly lavender scent of my mum's laundry. As my nose inhales the delicious aroma, a soft knock ripples across my door and my dad returns encouraging me to hurry up. After furiously brushing my teeth and sighing longingly at the shower I don't have time for, I flurry down the stairs to push on my sneakers.

"Where are we going?" I ask in between tying my laces.

"Just follow me."

We venture to our driveway out front. My dad inserts the car key into the driver door and tells me to get in. Diligently, I swing the passenger door ajar and take a seat. The car smells fusty from baking in the sun. The dense heat envelops my skin making me feel claustrophobic.

"So?" I turn and say to him as he buckles in behind the steering wheel and I wind the window down.

"We are going for a drive."

"I can see that, but where are we driving to exactly?"

He turns his face towards the road and pushes down on the acceleration, "Richmond."

"Richmond? Am I allowed to go to Richmond?"

"If we are back by 8 pm you are."

We edge away from my neighbourhood, and I watch the houses of the street grow ever smaller in the wing mirror. Where is Fred Andrews? I haven't noticed him or Janice since returning home. Has their marriage suffered since my allegations? If so – good. That's exactly what Fred deserves. Janice doesn't need a paedophile as a husband. Sophia doesn't need a paedophile as a father.

The road stretches straight beyond us now, a line of grey concrete fringed with the odd boxy shop and petrol station. The grass near the sidewalks is parched straw yellow. Although it isn't officially Summer, we've had weeks of sunshine and no rain. So I've heard at least. Within my peripheral vision, I catch my dad reaching for the radio. My fingers stop him from pressing the button. We need to talk before the insistent mumbling of music can drown out our thoughts.

"Where does mum think we are going?" I say, my eyes still fixated on the road.

"I left her a note. I worried if she knew what we were doing then she'd try and stop us but once we set off she couldn't intervene."

"What are we doing?"

I can tell by my dad's expression that he's ready to spill the beans. The question is, am I ready to hear it? He doesn't give me much time to prepare before he unleashes his secret.

"She accidentally ran someone over, back in Richmond, and Fred helped to cover it up. She's frightened that he'll expose her to the police if she confesses what's really going on behind closed doors."

My head can't stop shaking in dismay. I need to know one question, "Did they die? The person she ran over?"

Out of the corner of my eye, I watch as my dad's profile nods.

My eyes close tight and a groan escapes my lips. Forcefully, my clenched hand punches the side door of the car, and I recoil from the instant pain.

"Fuck!" I explode in response to the throbbing, and at the dire situation I find myself in, and at the revelation of Sophia's indiscretion. Who is this girl? Did I ever really know her? The whole state of affairs is so messed up. Ultimately, I'm fucked.

"I'm obviously going to let that language slide, given the context."

As my blood shimmers, doubt begins to set in.

"Why are we going to Richmond? What's the point?"

"I think we need to track down friends of Sophia and see what they can remember from the crash. Maybe they can attest to Fred's demeanour. She might have disclosed her abuse. Then we'd have witnesses to support our case." As my dad speaks I hang my head between my legs, this is such a lost cause. "It is worth a shot, Lucas. You're worth a shot," he declares sternly.

What have I got to lose? I sit back against my seat and smile a half-smile for just a split second. It is long enough for my dad to respond with a much larger and more positive grin. This time when his hand reaches for the radio dial, I let it turn. The car fills with the sounds of Motown and my father rhythmically tapping along to the beat. Having a plan, as dismal as the plan may be, cloaks me with a sense of optimism. The optimism is wafer thin, but it is there. Maybe, just maybe, we might be able to find a way out of this web of lies.

Chapter Nineteen

Route 80 stretches past Wildcat Canyon Regional Park. We speed beyond the dense acres of towering trees into the brick of City Central. My dad pulls up and unfolds a map for the dozenth time. His finger taps against 1402 Marina Way. It has already been circled with a black ball-point pen. I frown at his apparent preparation. Since when did my father become a detective?

We drive along Marina Way Street, and I see water glistening ahead with boat masts bobbing up and down. As we turn into a car park, my eyes squint to focus on a rounded man standing keenly in front of what looks to be a school.

"Is that...?"

"Mr Mathews tracked down Sophia's old High School. Wanted to help us best that he could," my father responds.

"Well, that is unexpected."

"He believes in you, Lucas. We all do."

The car doors bang shut as we leave the vehicle and steadfast towards Mr Mathews, who smiles broadly as we approach. It is strange to see him in more civilian clothing. All I've ever seen him wear are ill-fitting suits.

"Ready?" he asks, gesturing to the entrance of John Henry High School.

"Are we allowed to just go inside?" I question.

"I've already spoken to the Headmistress; they are expecting us and have organised for us to meet with two of Sophia's friends."

I can't believe how nice everyone is being. All my life, I've felt chastised by society somehow for seeing the world differently to people my age. Yet here I am, fighting for my livelihood, surrounded by like-minded individuals. Did I deserve such understanding?

"Are you coming, Lucas?" my father beckons, waving me through the school's doors.

Being a little past ten am, pupils are tucked away studying, making the halls eerily quiet. Our trio of feet taps against the varnished floor towards the Headmistress' office. She flings the door open to greet us before anyone can even signal our arrival.

"Boys, please come on in," she instructs. "Take a seat."

We oblige and sit on the chairs facing her large desk. Mr Mathews is the first to speak.

"Thank you for meeting with us. We promise not to take up too much of your time. As we discussed on the phone, speaking with Sophia's close friends could greatly help us exonerate Mr Stevenson."

I watch as he motions towards me, and the Headmistress' eyes rest on my face.

"Of course, anything to help. Sophia was a marvellous student, whatever her and Mr Stevenson are wrapped up in, I'm hopeful Ali and Trinity can support."

A tentative knock beats against the door behind us.

"Ah, here are the girls now."

As the Headmistress welcomes them in, I take my first glance at Sophia's joy-riding accomplices, and I am shocked at what I see. Neither of them appears as edgy or rebellious as I had imagined. They stand nervously in well-presented school uniform. No high-rise miniskirts or puffed-up collars insight. They aren't even wearing nail polish. Any indication of their personality, their real self, lay hidden away, behind their worried expressions.

"Now girls, you aren't in any trouble, these are not policeman, but what they do want to discuss with you today is very important. It is to do with your old friend, Sophia," the Headmistress explains.

Ali and Trinity turn to one another with mouths agape.

Mr Mathews coughs under his breath and flickers his eyes at the Headmistress, her name still unbeknown to me.

"I'll leave you to it. If you need anything I'll just be outside."

As soon as she leaves her office and closes the door, Ali and Trinity take a seat next to Mr Mathews.

"Is Sophia alright?" Ali pleads.

"Sophia is fine, it is Lucas whose freedom is in jeopardy." Mr Mathews looks the girls up and down as he speaks as if questioning their demeanour. As the girls screw their face up in confusion, I decide to interject.

"I'm Lucas by the way," I say with a wave despite their intimate proximity.

"So how does this involve Sophia?" Trinity chirps up, arms folded.

"What I am about to disclose is strictly confidential," Mr Mathews informs the girls before divulging the details. "Our client, Lucas, believes he witnessed Sophia's father abusing her.

Sophia is not supporting these claims. We think this is out of fear of her father."

My father twists his hands in his lap waiting for Ali or Trinity to react. I notice Ali's face of concern, whereas Trinity remains unfazed.

"That's terrible, how can we possibly help? We haven't seen Sophia since, since—"

"Go on," Mr Mathews encourages

"Since she left Richmond," Trinity finishes Ali's sentence off for her

"According to Sophia, you were interested in joy-riding back then. Is that correct?"

As Ali leans forward, like she is about the say something, Trinity holds her arm across Ali's torso. Stopping her

"Mrs Burckinghore says you aren't cops, why are you interested in that?" her voice airy and light.

"Because, Trinity, one of those car rides ended up in disaster, didn't it?"

Ali turns her head swiftly to glare at Trinity however Trinity's position does not change. She remains fixed to her chair, defiant and poised.

"You are wasting your time, we don't know what you are talking about," Trinity scoffs. "Come on Ali, we're leaving."

As the girls stand, Ali more slowly than Trinity, I see my father's desperate eyes grow large and intense. I too feel a pang in my heart. Our only shot wasted. The girls abruptly leave and in walks the Headmistress.

"Thank you for your cooperation Mrs Burckingshore," Mr Mathews expresses whilst shaking her hand.

"Of course, I do hope it helped."

We leave the school more sluggish than we once came. As we drag our feet back to the parking lot, hurried steps follow us.

"Wait!"

I snap my head around to follow the direction of the noise. Ali catches her breath as she stumbles nearer.

"I think I can help," she says, "but Trinity can't know, and you have to promise we won't get in trouble."

"Absolutely," Mr Mathews replies. "What can you tell us about the night of the accident?"

"I'm sure you know we were as high as a kite, driving around. Out of nowhere, we hear a bang and the car jolts to a stop. None of us dared to go out and take a look, but we knew we'd hit something."

As Ali speaks she rubs her right arm up and down. Comforting herself, I think.

"Go on," my dad urges.

"Well, that morning, after we returned to our homes, Mr Andrews came to my house."

"Fred Andrews, Sophia's dad?"

"Yes. He said that he knew what had happened and wanted to talk. I was petrified my parents would overhear, so I went with him," Ali reflects as she glances over her shoulder. "He told me to direct him to the scene of the accident. I managed to retrace our movements that night, and that's when we saw it."

The hair on my arms suddenly stands on end despite the warmth of the day. This is it.

"Mr Andrews, Frank, and I got out of the car to take a closer look. We noticed the dead deer by the side of the road. He made me help him dig a grave for it. It was awful."

"So you didn't kill a person?" I clarify.

"No! God no. I couldn't live with myself if we had."

"So why did you never report it? Why does Sophia not know you hit a deer?"

Ali was pulling at the skin on her arm now, making it grow red and sore.

"He said that he knew Trinity and I were in the car that night and that Sophia had said we were the ones that stole his car. He said Sophia told him Trinity was the one driving and she was angry with us both. He threatened to press charges if we ever hung out with his daughter again."

We all glance at each other in amazement. Relief drains from my body. Sophia isn't a killer. Fred has nothing on her.

"Ali, this has been incredibly helpful. Would you go on record with this statement? You won't face any penalties, I promise. You are a witness, not a criminal."

"…I'm not sure. If Trinity finds out… her parents are worse than mine. They would kick her out if they knew what we were up to."

I reach out and grab Ali's hand.

"Please, Ali, please, without your help I could go to jail and Sophia will stay living with a father who rapes her."

"Rapes!"

"Yes."

Seconds pass and Ali takes a long exhale, finally letting go.

"Okay, if you can promise Trinity and I won't face any charges, I'll do whatever you need."

Chapter Twenty

A frenzy of giddiness flows over me. On the car ride back home, I cannot refrain from fidgeting in my seat. My nerve endings fire with electricity, my skin quivers with building anticipation. The half-smile I forced across my face earlier this morning is now replaced with an uncontrollable grin. I will the car to move faster – closer to salvation.

"You're like an excitable toddler," my dad comments.

"I just can't wait to tell Sophia," I beam.

He suddenly eases off the pedal and turns towards me with a serious expression.

"Lucas, you can't see Sophia. You are still on bail. You must obey the rules of your tag. We aren't out of the woods yet. Don't do anything to jeopardise this."

Turns out the smirk can be wiped from my face. I shake my head defiantly, unable to verbally concede to my father's orders.

"Let Mr Mathews do his thing and let's see what the outcome is, hey," he suggests while patting my jerking leg, "today is a good day."

He is right. I just can't disguise the pulsating desire to be the one to salvage everything. Never in my life did I think I'd play the role of a hero, and now I have the title – almost, and I can't even get the satisfaction of seeing it unfold in real-time. As a guy that has been closed off from the world for weeks, this is agonisingly difficult to accept. I want to reclaim myself, my life, my way - the only way I know how. Except for this time, I won't seek the unknown or unseen. I will venture into the dark to reveal the truth. A truth that I hope will set us all free.

"Where have you been?" Mum shouts as dad and I walk through the front door. She places her hand on her hip, emphasising her point.

"Didn't you get my note?" dad asks nonchalantly.

"Don't play coy with me, you're up to something."

We glance at one another with a knowing agreeance only family members can detect. Dad tells her about the details surrounding our trip, and after a few groans and moans, she's soon bursting at the seams with joy.

"You mean..."

"Mr Mathews says we can't get our hopes up, but he feels pretty positive it will be enough to change Sophia's testimony."

Her arms drag me into an embrace, and my face squishes against her ribcage.

"So what do we do now? How long will it take for him to speak with the Police?"

"He's on his way there now."

Chapter Twenty-One

Night takes an eternity to come. Now the sun has finally set, I sliver out of my house. If I dawdle, I may not have enough time to make it to Sophia before the police arrive. That doesn't stop me sucking in the evening air with exhilaration and fondness. My nocturnal surroundings seem to acknowledge my presence approvingly. How I've missed you.

My dad is mistaken. By the time the cops come, they'll have been notified with Ali's statement and Sophia will have been unburdened from the lies, empowered to fight against her father once and for all. Things will all work out, he'll see.

I pierce the familiar key into Sophia's front door, but it resists. I force it again and again without success. Damn it, the key no longer fits. As I stand contemplating my next move, the hallway floods with light. Abruptly, the door flings open to reveal Janice, tired-eyed and enraged.

"What are you doing here?"

"I need to speak with Sophia. It's urgent."

"I don't care how urgent it is, you aren't supposed to be here."

"Sophia!" I call, storming past Janice. My feet fly up the stairs as Janice calls me back. I ignore her cries and run into Sophia's room.

"Sophia, I need to talk to you."

As I rush over to her bed, I see it is empty.

"Where is she? Has he got her?" I press.

"Has who got her?"

As I turn round, I already know who is hovering by the doorway – Fred Andrews. Wrapped in a dressing gown he rubs his eyes and glares at me. Janice stands behind him watching on with worry.

"Where is Sophia?" Janice screams. "Where has she gone?"

A blare of sirens interrupts her outburst, and I falter with my steps. What's happening?

"I think you better be going," Fred declares. "They're coming for you."

I scan Sophia's room one last time and notice her opened, empty drawers. My stomach drops and a lump forms in my throat. I'm too late.

Bounding down the stairs, the shrieks elevate in my ears. My parents are already stood on the pavement, concern plastered across their weary faces.

"Lucas, what did I say," my dad scorns when I walk outside.

"Sophia's missing."

"What?" my mum replies.

Just then, I hear the sound of car doors creak open and then slam shut. Before I can respond, a police officer grabs my arm and leads me into the back of his patrol car. Outside the car window, I hear the muffled voice of Janice begging the officers to find her daughter. To find Sophia. Fred loiters in the background, quiet. Just as we are about to speed off to the station, I think I see him begin to cry.

Chapter Twenty-Two

My heels dig into the station's floor with the sound of every footstep and slammed door. To be here, again. My head slumps in shame. I focus on the thump of my heart, beating with the velocity of a hummingbird.

Sophia's gone.

The room's door flings open, startling me from my stupor.

"You're bloody lucky to have me, boy," Mr Mathews asserts.

He grinds a chair out from under the table and sits to face me. A peculiar laugh erupts from his smiling mouth.

"What's going on?"

"Surprisingly, Fred has dropped all charges against you and revised his statement," he muses.

My brows wrinkle with uncertainty.

"What, how?"

"Like I said, you are lucky to have me. Turns out Fred is easy to shake when confronted with the truth. He's a clever man, knows what's good for him. Knows he has no leverage. Especially when I said that all we needed to do was find the burial site to disprove his claims."

So Mathews spoke to Fred. Revealed our ace card. If only I could have been there to see the colour drain from his skin.

"You told him about Ali's statement?" I clarify.

"I told him that we had witnesses of our own but thought best to leave names out of it. We've muddied the waters enough the cast suspicion, but the police don't have enough to convict Fred, without Sophia."

My eyes settle on the plastic table in front of me. If only she'd have waited before running away. Fred could be behind bars by now.

"No sign of her then?"

"Nothing," he says while shaking his head. "I'm sorry."

She is out there somewhere, still believing that she killed someone, still afraid of her father. A man I now owe my freedom to. The thought leaves a bad taste in my mouth.

"So... what's next for me?"

"Given your age and lack of witnesses and testimony, you're being let off with a fine – mainly for breaking your bail terms." The way he says the latter end of his sentence indicates that he's still pretty pissed at me for doing that. I best alter the course of this conversation.

"Thanks for everything," I applaud. "Really. It wouldn't have panned out like this without you."

I stretch out my hand to shake Mr Mathews. Although the prospect of prison is behind me, no one is better off than when we first started. You could argue things are worse. A sordid thought crosses my mind. Would life be better if I'd have just left the secrets undisturbed, in the dark?

Chapter Twenty-Three

It is strange to think that I miss boring, humdrum suburban life in Roseville. Technically, we only moved 5 miles down the road, so we are still in Roseville, but it isn't the same Roseville that I grew up in.

Our new house is positioned on the corner of an estate with views over Diamond Oaks golfing range. My dad loves the nearby amenities. My mum misses the slightly shorter commute to work. Some nights, I forget where I am and peer out of my window hoping to see Sophia's house starring back at me, but no. It is just the golfing green now. Acres of bottle green flatland.

I spend my days in a perpetual daze. I can't move forwards, and as much as I long to, I can't go back. I try to focus on the single most important thing in my life now – photography.

"Ready skipper?" my dad says as he opens my bedroom door, no knocking required.

I shake my camera. "Let's go."

We drive out to Folsom Lake, our Sunday morning ritual, coffee mug in hand. An autumn air swamps the vista like steam, muting all the forest shades. The lake's brilliant blue is now tinged grey – it has lost its summer sparkle. The path crunches underfoot as I snap pictures all around us, attempting to capture the sombre haze with some semblance of skill.

Without the sound of distant crickets and bird song, the place would be silent.

"Up there," my father whispers, pointing to a nearby tree.

I zoom in on a Finch perched on a spindly branch. It turns its black head towards me. It looks straight into my camera lens before soaring off into the frosty mist. My aperture captures the entire moment until it is gone.

I live for these days. If nothing else, recent experiences have brought me closer to my father. We understand how one another feels, without having to discuss it.

We circle back to the car, eager to return for one of mum's decadent weekend breakfasts. Inside, I close my eyes and focus on the melodies of the radio. I can tell exactly where we are on the journey just by the feeling of the terrain. The smoothness of our new street unfolds, and we slow our pace to a stop.

I amble inside to the aroma of floury pancakes and sweet syrup. I'd drown my plate in the golden liquid if my mum would allow.

Afterwards, my parents ask if I'd like to join them in visiting Francis. I don't. With nothing to do but enjoy having the house to myself, I peruse my library of books. Which one will keep me company? Oscar Wilde, Mark Twain, George Orwell?

My fingers land on the worn spine of Gabriel Garcia Marquez.

Book in tandem, I return to bed and my eyes begin to read: *Many years later, as he faced the firing squad, Colonel Aureliano Buendía was to remember that distant afternoon when his father took him to discover ice.*

Some way into the pages, I lose track of the words. My eyes fight to stay open until I can no longer compete. Sleep wins.

A feeling of warmth covers my body. The scent of tropical flowers pervades. I lick my lips instinctively. Soft tresses float across the skin of my cheeks and neck, so lifelike that I swat them away. Is that? It can't be?

My eyes flash open. Her face lingers over mine. Her chalk-white skin like a star of light against the shadowy surroundings.

"Sophia," I breathe.

"Shhh," she hushes as she places a finger against my lip. She slowly removes it, caressing the folds of my mouth as she moves. Through all the questions whirling through my brain, a feeling overpowers. I clasp her head in my hands and bring her mouth to mine with a hard, desperate kiss.

"Where have you been?" I murmur against her lips.

"I've been following you. How does it feel?"

"But —"

"We can talk later," she mutters as she slides beneath my sheets. "Just for now, can this be enough?"

We eventually untangle our entwined bodies, exhausted and exhilarated all at the same time.

I turn my body lengthways to meet her perfect, flushed face. My head props up against my palm. "You never killed anyone, Sophia. It was all a lie."

"What?" she asks. Her voice more an exhale than words. A crease deepens between her brows, and I notice tears forming in the inner corners of her closed eyes.

I tell her everything I know. The visit to Ali and Trinity, the deer, the ultimatum.

She holds her hand up abruptly. "Stop... I can't hear anymore."

I encase her body in the shields of my arms, and pull her head into the nape of my naked neck, considering how hard it must be to discover your life had been a lie. That you never needed to make such horrendous choices.

"I'm so sorry," my mouth speaks against her wild hair. I failed her, too. "I thought I'd lost you forever after what I did."

Sophia opens her wistful gaze to mine. "You set me free. For that I thank you. In fact, I... I love you."

"I love you, too."

I stop talking, stop thinking and sink into the feeling of Sophia between my arms. The enigmatic girl that stole my heart, and beat me at my own game.

Work by Hollie

LoveSick
The Silver Lining